SELECTED VERSE

RUDYARD KIPLING

SELECTED VERSE

With an introduction by
LIZZY WELBY

MACMILLAN COLLECTOR'S LIBRARY

This edition first published by Collector's Library 2012

Reissued by Macmillan Collector's Library 2016
an imprint of Pan Macmillan
20 New Wharf Road, London N1 9RR
Associated companies throughout the world
www.panmacmillan.com

ISBN 978-1-909621-83-1

1 3 5 7 9 8 6 4 2

A CIP catalogue record for this book is available from the British Library.

Typeset by Antony Gray
Printed and bound in China by Imago

Visit www.panmacmillan.com to read more about all our books
and to buy them. You will also find features, author interviews and
news of any author events, and you can sign up for e-newsletters
so that you're always first to hear about our new releases.

Contents

Introduction

DR LIZZY WELBY

Rudyard Kipling's art, like the man himself, is curiously kaleidoscopic. Just as you think you have understood him, you stumble across a piece he has penned that sends you scuttling back to square one. Taking a broad view of his writing career, which spanned more than five decades (six, if you include the posthumous publications), you will find a broad range of writing, from novels and short stories to propaganda speeches and iconic inscriptions for the War Graves Commission. He could write for adults and children with equal deftness and imbue animals and machines with an authentic voice. Alongside his prose, Kipling is equally well known for his verse, all of which seems almost effortless in its technical accomplishment, including the notoriously complex sestina. At a young age, he could parody, in voice, tone and technique great poets on both sides of the Atlantic, from Milton to Emerson, Wordsworth to Stevenson. And the door swings both ways. Kipling's influence can be read in T. S. Eliot's poetry[1] (he

---

1 When addressing members of the Kipling Society at their Annual Luncheon, Eliot stated that 'Kipling had accompanied me ever since boyhood [and] traces of [his art] appear in my own mature verse where no diligent scholarly sleuth has yet observed them'. 'The Unfading Genius of Rudyard Kipling', *Kipling Journal*, vol. 36, 129, 1959, 9–12 (p. 9). Robert Crawford has subsequently tracked down some of those traces of Kipling in Eliot's

borrowed the metre from 'The Long Trail' for 'Skimbleshanks the Railway Cat', in his *Old Possum's Book of Practical Cats*). From earliest years, Kipling flitted between worlds and across class and race divides and his diverse experiences (as well as those of the many people he encountered along the way) were filtered and refracted though his art.

Over the years, Kipling has simultaneously infuriated and captivated his readers. His much-anthologized 'If —', perhaps his most famous verse, certainly voted the 'Nation's Favourite Twentieth Century Poem' by a long chalk, epitomises the man and his art. Undone by its own success, it has been quoted to cliché yet it remains a clarion call for resilience when situations are difficult. It was used at political rallies by Burmese dissident Aung San Suu Kyi, scratched onto the prison wall of feisty Latin American women tortured after Pinochet's coup and apparently committed to memory by Che Guevara. Clearly, as T. S. Eliot thought, along with Angus Wilson and latterly Harry Ricketts, this is a writer worth rescuing from a literary wasteland.

The diverse subjects, which Kipling tackled through a range of voices and styles, has, inevitably split opinions down the years. His critics could (and did) depict him as youthful aesthetic or tub-thumping Tory, Imperial apologist or critic of Empire,

---

poetry. For his excellent analysis of Kipling's influence on Eliot's work see Robert Crawford, 'Rudyard Kipling in *The Waste Land*', *Essays in Criticism*, vol. 36, 1, 1986, 32–46.

ethnocentric globetrotter or culture-embracing traveler, anti-Liberal spokesperson or voice of the marginalized, Fabulist, Realist, Symbolist or early Modernist, to name just a few of the tags that have been attached to this writer who simply refuses to sink into obscurity. Generally, critics agree on two constants that wove their conflicting way through the fabric of Kipling's life and profoundly informed his writing: India, birthplace and first home, and England, birthright and 'Home'. I came late to Kipling, exchanging my working life for study as my family began to expand. *The Jungle Book* provided bedtime reading for my growing son and I was intrigued to see him sense the sorrow that lies at the heart of the orphan 'man-cub' forced to choose between two incompatible worlds.

The ambivalence that lies at the heart of Kipling's verse and prose was, I believe, forged in childhood. Across the decades in his autobiography, India is remembered as a vibrant noisy country, backlit with sharp sunshine and soft sunset hues, an edenic space filled with a host of solicitous servants, a devoted *ayah* and two loving parents.[2] Just short of his sixth birthday, however, Kipling and his three-year old sister Trix boarded a boat in Bombay bound for England with their parents Alice and Lockwood. After a short stay with various relatives, the children were taken to a boarding house in Southsea. Without

2 Rudyard Kipling, *Something of Myself and Other Autobiographical Writings*, ed. by Thomas Pinney, Cambridge, Cambridge University Press, 1991, pp. 4–5.

a word of her imminent departure, Alice stole away to join her husband in London before sailing back to Bombay, leaving her infant children in the care of Sarah Holloway, fervent evangelical and owner of Lorne Lodge, which Kipling was to later term the 'House of Desolation'. Six years would pass before either of them saw their mother again. 'Father in Heaven who lovest all, / Oh, help Thy children when they call;/ That they may build from age to age / An undefiled heritage', writes Kipling in 'The Children's Song' in 1906 and there is more than an echo of his lost youth in its lines.

Every Christmas little Ruddy exchanged his grey Southsea prison for The Grange, the wonderful Fulham home of his Aunt Georgie and Uncle Ned, the Pre-Raphaelite painter Edward Burne-Jones. There he roamed freely with much-loved cousins, laid claim to a special mulberry tree for 'plots and conferences', glimpsed newly created Pre-Raphaelite art and furniture and listened to William Morris, 'Uncle Topsy', recite Icelandic Sagas while swaying rhythmically back and forth atop a rocking horse. His beloved aunty would read Scott's *The Pirate* or *The Arabian Nights*. The Grange was, by the author's account, a 'jumble of delights and emotions'.[3] There is much in the happy disorder that characterised the Burne-Jones' home that found its thematic way into his prose and verse. '*The Weald is good, the Downs are best – / I'll give you the run of 'em, East to West*' promises the author to his fictional children Dan and

3 *Something of Myself*, pp. 9–10.

Una, in 'The Run of the Downs'. Life at The Grange flowed like the 'broad smiling river of life' on the Grand Trunk Road in *Kim* and the same delight appears in verses such as 'Mandalay' where memories of India are sensually evoked in 'them spicy garlic smells, /An' the sunshine an' the palm-trees an' the tinkly temple-bells'.

With such an immersion into the creative life of the artist, it is of little surprise that from his early teens Kipling displayed a precocious talent for writing, particularly verse. It was a talent encouraged and nurtured by Cormell Price, headmaster of the United Services College in Westward Ho! where Kipling passed his school years. 'Uncle Crom', as he was affectionately known, was a family friend with Pre-Raphaelite connections and an aesthete. It was he who accompanied Ruddy on his journey to the 'twelve bleak houses' at a windswept Bideford Bay. 'Ave Imperatrix!' (a parody of though markedly different from Oscar Wilde's vision of the death of Imperialism) was written when Kipling was a pupil at USC. Most likely written in tongue-in-cheek tones, it nevertheless anticipates much of the momentous verse that Kipling would go on to write such as 'Recessional' that, in its portentous stanzas, quietly signaled to the 'flannelled fools at the wicket' that their eternal British Empire would soon reach its closing overs.

Despite achieving such early success, no one could predict that this young cub of a journalist, feverishly churning out short fiction to fill the 'turnover' space of Lahore's *Civil and Military Gazette*, would go on to world fame, pulling off the rare trick of appealing to a popular audience as well as a literary one. By the age of twenty-three, he had already published two slim volumes of verse, seven collections of short stories, including *Plain Tales From the Hills* and a host of travel sketches, later collected as the 'Letters of Marque' in *From Sea to Sea*. The ripples he was causing in London literary circles would quickly widen out across the globe, helped along by the modernization of a book-making industry to cater for a new global demand. Mark Twain was to remark famously that Kipling was 'the only living person not head of a nation, whose voice is heard around the world the moment it drops a remark'. Yet a mere two decades later he had suffered the loss of his 'best beloved' daughter Josephine from pneumonia in 1899 (the original recipient of the *Just So* stories), of his best friend and collaborator on *The Naulahka*, Wolcott Balestier, to whom *Barrack-Room Ballads* is dedicated and of his son John at the Battle of the Loos in 1915. In addition, Kipling's artistic reputation and apparent perennial success, was on the wane.

Some of Kipling's critics had always been uneasy with the verse and prose shot through with political polemic, undisguised enjoyment of cruelty and revenge, and masculine bravado. But by 1918 the wider public had lost its taste for flag-flapping verses like 'The White Man's Burden'. Kipling's patriotic bluster, epitomized in verses like 'A Song of the English' and 'For All We Have and Are', blew itself out at the end of the First World War, although he reserved the right to pen periodically what he saw as an ever-present German menace, perfectly captured in 'The Storm Cone', until the end of his life. Once billed as the Imperial Bard, Kipling had little to offer in the way of consolation for a nation still reeling in profound shock from the horrors of modern warfare that had devoured a generation of its young men. 'A world to be remade without a son' said his wife Carrie as the war guttered to its end.[4] John's body was never found in the Kiplings' lifetime and 'My Boy Jack', an in absentia requiem hymn, sees their vanished son ghost across its lines. Rudyard's contrition for the part he played in speeding his myopic son up the lines to Armageddon is just as poignant in 'Epitaphs of War', 'If any question why we died, / Tell them, because our fathers lied'. A new breed of writers, bereft of the mainstays of Victorian mores, were busy detailing the spiritual paralysis of a post-war England. Receding hairlines and kidney breakfasts now occupied the psyches of new Modernist heroes and it seemed certain that Kipling would be consigned to history as irretrievably passé.

The Imperial world that Kipling charted, the workers of Empire he championed and their unsung deeds he highlighted began to vanish as silence settled over France's blood-silted battlefields. Yet poems published in the last two decades of the nineteenth century such as 'Danny Deever', 'Tommy' and 'Private Ortheris's Song' are concerned with the

4 Quoted in, Harry Ricketts, *The Unforgiving Minute: A Life of Rudyard Kipling*, London, Chatto & Windus, 1999, p. 340.

ordinary soldier's (miserably unappreciated) lot, a theme that would be subsequently taken up by poets of the First World War. Kipling always championed the ordinary soldier. Verses such as 'Gentlemen-Ranker', 'The Broken Men', 'Tommy', 'The Absent Minded-Beggar', 'Gunga Din' and 'Fuzzy-Wuzzy' as well as 'The Grave of the Hundred Head' laud those men, British or 'native', charged with guarding colonial borders. The much mis-quoted 'The Ballad of East and West' valorises courage, strength and resource-fulness that cut across cultural borders. South African verse such as 'The Settler' has the tone, not of vitriolic finger-pointing, but of reconciliation. The unrelenting metronomic rhythm of 'Boots', written during the Boer War, expresses the strain of soldiers engaged in combat:

> Try–try–try–try–to think o' something different –
> Oh–my–God–keep–me from goin' lunatic!
> (Boots–boots–boots–boots–movin' up an' down
>   again!)
>   There's no discharge in the war!

British and American soldiers are once again marching through the unforgiving terrain of Afghanistan, experiencing the same psychological unease that 'Ford O' Kabul River' captures so menacingly:

> Ford o' Kabul river in the dark!
> Gawd 'elp 'em if they blunder, for their boots'll
>   pull 'em under,
> By the ford o' Kabul river in the dark.

Kipling was always critical of the automated bureaucracy of Empire that was responsible for battle-worn soldiers, fevered engineers and overworked administrators being posted to far-flung corners of the globe, just as he always extolled the individual's courage, dedication and endurance in seemingly impossible situations, attributes he considered to be the cornerstone of integrity. Men (and occasionally women) can find meaning in the Imperial project but Empire is made worthy by the deeds of individuals, typified in 'The Law of the Jungle', 'the strength of the Pack is the Wolf, and the strength of the Wolf is the Pack'.

My own interest in Kipling's work lies in an exploration of the 'feminine' form. Some of his verse and prose is imbued with a tenderness for and fear of a 'lost' maternal realm. For example, 'The Deep-Sea Cables' that sings of a time before a masculine order and calls for an embracing of the feminine within.

> Here in the womb of the world - here on the tie-
> ribs of earth
> Words, and the words of men, flicker and flutter
> and beat –
> [. . .]
> They have wakened the timeless Things; They
> have killed their father Time
> [. . .]
> And a new Word runs between: whispering, 'Let
> us be one!'

More than six decades later three female French academics would begin exploring the idea of a female voice that is inserted into the gap that runs between the pre-verbal maternal realm and the language of men. And there it is, right here in this extraordinary poem. The beautifully crafted 'Harp Song of the Dane Women' is a haunting lament for absent seafarers. In iambic tetrameter, which reflects the ebb and flow of sea-tides (and, incidentally, is the rhythmic heartbeat of ballads), and using vocabulary that is Anglo-Saxon in origin, we understand the irresistible call of the treacherous sea luring sailors to her steely waters:

> She has no strong white arms to fold you,
> But the ten-times-fingering weed to hold you –
> Out on the rocks where the tide has rolled you.
>
> Yet, when the signs of summer thicken,
> And the ice breaks, and the birch-buds quicken,
> Yearly you turn from our side, and sicken –

The feminized sea is to be found again in 'The Sea and the Hills' and her pull is just as mesmeric but this time the calming maternal presence of the land is longed for, too. Gems like these, hidden in a body of work that at times makes one wince, are why Kipling's art refuses to fade. These lesser known pieces deserves restoration, not least to counter less praiseworthy verses such as 'The Female of the Species', 'The Vampire' or 'The Betrothed', the latter containing the lines, oft-quoted axiomatically by the male of the species, 'a woman is only a woman, but a good Cigar is a Smoke'.

Kipling spent his final years at Bateman's in Sussex, a little corner of a foreign field that a restless

Anglo-Indian came to finally call home, 'Here through the strong and shadeless days / The tinkling silence thrills' he wrote in 'Sussex'. Over time the rolling Downs meant as much to him as his much-loved Indian homeland. He once wrote that 'history understood [sic] rightly means love of one's fellow men and the lands they live in'.[5] To introduce the *Rewards and Fairies* collection, Kipling gives us 'A Charm'. In its verses we see his 'new' England, a welcoming pluralist pastoral where every inhabitant becomes a symbolic custodian of Britain's ancient heritage, a heritage that is bound, not to the ideology of a governing body but to the land:

> Take of English earth as much
> As either hand may rightly clutch.
> In the taking of it breathe
> Prayer for all who lie beneath.
> Not the great nor well-bespoke,
> But the mere uncounted folk
> Of whose life and death is none
> Report or lamentation.
> Lay that earth upon thy heart,
> And thy sickness shall depart!

In this varied selection of verses you will undoubtedly find the Kipling that you always knew but I hope that you will also find the Kipling who might just, until now, have lain hidden from you.

5 Rudyard Kipling to Edward Bok, July 1905 in *The Letters of Rudyard Kipling*, Iowa City, University of Iowa Press, 1990–96, p, 189.

Further Reading

Charles Allen, *Kipling Sahib: India and The Making of Rudyard Kipling*, London, Little Brown, 2007

David Gilmou , *The Long Recessional: The Imperial Life of Rudyard Kipling*, London, John Murray, 2002

Harry Ricketts, *The Unforgiving Minute: A Life of Rudyard Kipling*, London, Chatto & Windus, 1999

Angus Wilson, *The Strange Ride of Rudyard Kipling: His Life and Works*, London, Secker & Warburg, 1977

Biography

Rudyard Kipling (1865–1936) was born in Bombay, but at the age of six was sent to live with foster parents in England. This was a wretched period of his life for he was bullied and ill-treated by those who were supposed to be caring for him. When he was twelve he went to the United Services College at Westward Ho! near Bideford in Devon, an establishment that specialised in training boys for a military life. However, Kipling's poor eyesight and his mediocre academic achievements ruled out any hope of a successful career in the forces. Nevertheless, one good thing did come out of his time at the college: the headmaster, Cormell Price, a friend of his father, fostered his literary abilities.

In 1882, Kipling returned to India, where he worked for the *Civil and Military Gazette* in Lahore and other Anglo-Indian newspapers. At this time he also began to write fiction. He was a prolific writer and achieved fame quickly. In 1894 *The Jungle Book* appeared and became a children's classic all over the world. Kipling's later life was blighted by tragedy: in 1899 his elder daughter Josephine died of influenza and in 1915 his only son, John, was killed in the Battle of Loos.

Kipling was one of the most popular writers in English in both prose and verse in the late nineteenth and early twentieth centuries. The author Henry James said of him: 'Kipling strikes me personally as the most complete man of genius . . . that I have ever known.'

In 1907 Kipling was awarded the Nobel Prize for Literature, making him the first English-language writer to receive the award, and he remains the youngest ever recipient. Among other honours, he was sounded out for the post of Poet Laureate and on several occasions for a knighthood, both of which he declined. Apart from *Kim* and the other titles referred to, his works include: *Plain Tales from the Hills* (1888); *Soldiers Three* (1888); *Captains Courageous* (1897); *Stalky & Co* (1899); *Just So Stories* (1902) and *Puck of Pook's Hill* (1906); and his collected poems, which appeared in 1933.

SELECTED VERSE OF
RUDYARD KIPLING

Prelude to 'Departmental Ditties'

I have eaten your bread and salt.
   I have drunk your water and wine.
The deaths ye died I have watched beside,
   And the lives ye led were mine.

Was there aught that I did not share
   In vigil or toil or ease, –
One joy or woe that I did not know,
   Dear hearts across the seas?

I have written the tale of our life
   For a sheltered people's mirth,
In jesting guise – but ye are wise,
   And ye know what the jest is worth.

1885

The Story of Uriah

'Now there were two men in one city;
the one rich, and the other poor.'

Jack Barrett went to Quetta
  Because they told him to.
He left his wife at Simla
  On three-fourths his monthly screw.
Jack Barrett died at Quetta
  Ere the next month's pay he drew.

Jack Barrett went to Quetta.
  He didn't understand
The reason of his transfer
  From the pleasant mountain-land.
The season was September,
  And it killed him out of hand.

Jack Barrett went to Quetta
  And there gave up the ghost,
Attempting two men's duty
  In that very healthy post;
And Mrs Barrett mourned for him
  Five lively months at most.

Jack Barrett's bones at Quetta
  Enjoy profound repose;
But I shouldn't be astonished
  If *now* his spirit knows
The reason of his transfer
  From the Himalayan snows.

And, when the Last Great Bugle Call
    Adown the Hurnai throbs,
And the last grim joke is entered
    In the big black Book of Jobs,
And Quetta graveyards give again
    Their victims to the air,
I shouldn't like to be the man
    Who sent Jack Barrett there.

The Post that Fitted

Though tangled and twisted the course of true love,
This ditty explains,
No tangle's so tangled it cannot improve
If the Lover has brains.

Ere the steamer bore him Eastward, Sleary was
    engaged to marry
An attractive girl at Tunbridge, whom he called
    'my little Carrie.'
Sleary's pay was very modest; Sleary was the other
    way.
Who can cook a two-plate dinner on eight poor
    rupees a day?

Long he pondered o'er the question in his scantly
    furnished quarters –
Then proposed to Minnie Boffkin, eldest of Judge
    Boffkin's daughters.
Certainly an impecunious Subaltern was not a
    catch,
But the Boffkins knew that Minnie mightn't make
    another match.

So they recognised the business and, to feed and
    clothe the bride,
Got him made a Something Something somewhere
    on the Bombay side.
Anyhow, the billet carried pay enough for him to
    marry –
As the artless Sleary put it: – 'Just the thing for me
    and Carrie.'

Did he, therefore, jilt Miss Boffkin – impulse of a
    baser mind?
No! He started epileptic fits of an appalling kind.
[Of his *modus operandi* only this much I could
    gather: –
'Pears's shaving sticks will give you little taste and
    lots of lather.']

Frequently in public places his affliction used to
    smite
Sleary with distressing vigour – always in the
    Boffkins' sight.
Ere a week was over Minnie weepingly returned
    his ring,
Told him his 'unhappy weakness' stopped all
    thought of marrying.

Sleary bore the information with a chastened holy
    joy, –
Epileptic fits don't matter in Political employ, –
Wired three short words to Carrie – took his
    ticket, packed his kit –
Bade farewell to Minnie Boffkin in one last, long,
    lingering fit.

Four weeks later, Carrie Sleary read – and
    laughed until she wept –
Mrs Boffkin's warning letter on the 'wretched
    epilept.' . . .
Year by year, in pious patience, vengeful Mrs
    Boffkin sits
Waiting for the Sleary babies to develop Sleary's
    fits.

The Overland Mail

Foot-service to the Hills

In the Name of the Empress of India, make way,
   O Lords of the Jungle, wherever you roam,
The woods are astir at the close of the day –
   We exiles are waiting for letters from Home.
Let the robber retreat – let the tiger turn tail –
In the Name of the Empress, the Overland Mail!

With a jingle of bells as the dusk gathers in,
   He turns to the footpath that heads up the hill –
The bags on his back and a cloth round his chin,
   And, tucked in his waistbelt, the Post Office bill: –
'Despatched on this date, as received by the rail,
Per runner, two bags of the Overland Mail.'

Is the torrent in spate? He must ford it or swim.
   Has the rain wrecked the road? He must climb
   by the cliff.
Does the tempest cry halt? What are tempests to
   him?
   The service admits not a 'but' or an 'if'.
While the breath's in his mouth, he must bear
   without fail,
In the Name of the Empress, the Overland Mail.

From aloe to rose-oak, from rose-oak to fir,
   From level to upland, from upland to crest,
From rice-field to rock-ridge, from rock-ridge to
   spur,
   Fly the soft-sandalled feet, strains the brawny,
     brown chest.
From rail to ravine – to the peak from the vale –
Up, up through the night goes the Overland Mail.

There's a speck on the hillside, a dot on the road –
　　A jingle of bells on the footpath below –
There's a scuffle above in the monkey's abode –
　　The world is awake and the clouds are aglow.
For the great Sun himself must attend to the hail: –
'In the Name of the Empress, the Overland Mail!'

The Betrothed

'You must choose between me and your cigar.'
Breach of Promise Case, *c.*1885

Open the old cigar-box, get me a Cuba stout,
For things are running crossways, and Maggie and
I are out.

We quarrelled about Havanas – we fought o'er a
good cheroot,
And *I* know she is exacting, and she says I am a
brute.

Open the old cigar-box – let me consider a space;
In the soft blue veil of the vapour musing on
Maggie's face.

Maggie is pretty to look at – Maggie's a loving
lass,
But the prettiest cheeks must wrinkle, the truest of
loves must pass.

There's peace in a Larranaga, there's calm in a
Henry Clay;
But the best cigar in an hour is finished and
thrown away –

Thrown away for another as perfect and ripe and
brown –
But I could not throw away Maggie for fear o' the
talk o' the town!

Maggie, my wife at fifty – grey and dour and old –
With never another Maggie to purchase for love
or gold!

And the light of Days that have Been the dark of
    the Days that Are,
And Love's torch stinking and stale, like the butt
    of a dead cigar –

The butt of a dead cigar you are bound to keep in
    your pocket –
With never a new one to light tho' it's charred and
    black to the socket!

Open the old cigar-box – let me consider a while.
Here is a mild Manila – there is a wifely smile.

Which is the better portion – bondage bought
    with a ring,
Or a harem of dusky beauties, fifty tied in a string?

Counsellors cunning and silent – comforters true
    and tried,
And never a one of the fifty to sneer at a rival bride?

Thought in the early morning, solace in time of
    woes,
Peace in the hush of the twilight, balm ere my
    eyelids close,

This will the fifty give me, asking nought in
    return,
With only a *Suttee's* passion – to do their duty and
    burn.

This will the fifty give me. When they are spent
    and dead,
Five times other fifties shall be my servants
    instead.

The furrows of far-off Java, the isles of the
      Spanish Main,
When they hear my harem is empty will send me
      my brides again.

I will take no heed to their raiment, nor food for
      their mouths withal,
So long as the gulls are nesting, so long as the
      showers fall.

I will scent 'em with best vanilla, with tea will I
      temper their hides,
And the Moor and the Mormon shall envy who
      read of the tale of my brides.

For Maggie has written a letter to give me my
      choice between
The wee little whimpering Love and the great god
      Nick o' Teen.

And I have been servant of Love for barely a
      twelvemonth clear,
But I have been Priest of Cabanas a matter of
      seven year;

And the gloom of my bachelor days is flecked with
      the cheery light
Of stumps that I burned to Friendship and
      Pleasure and Work and Fight.

And I turn my eyes to the future that Maggie and
      I must prove,
But the only light on the marshes is the Will-o'-
      the-Wisp of Love.

Will it see me safe through my journey or leave
    me bogged in the mire?
Since a puff of tobacco can cloud it, shall I follow
    the fitful fire?

Open the old cigar-box – let me consider anew –
Old friends, and who is Maggie that I should
    abandon *you*?

A million surplus Maggies are willing to bear the
    yoke;
And a woman is only a woman, but a good Cigar
    is a Smoke.

Light me another Cuba – I hold to my first-sworn
    vows.
If Maggie will have no rival, I'll have no Maggie
    for Spouse!

The Grave of the Hundred Head

There's a widow in sleepy Chester.
  Who weeps for her only son;
There's a grave on the Pabeng River,
  A grave that the Burmans shun;
And there's Subadar Prag Tewarri
  Who tells how the work was done.

A Snider squibbed in the jungle –
  Somebody laughed and fled,
And the men of the First Shikaris
  Picked up their Subaltern dead,
With a big blue mark in his forehead
  And the back blown out of his head.

Subadar Prag Tewarri,
  Jemadar Hira Lal,
Took command of the party,
  Twenty rifles in all,
Marched them down to the river
  As the day was beginning to fall.

They buried the boy by the river,
  A blanket over his face –
They wept for their dead Lieutenant,
  The men of an alien race –
They made a *samadh* in his honour,
  A mark for his resting-place.

For they swore by the Holy Water,
  They swore by the salt they ate,
That the soul of Lieutenant Eshmitt Sahib
  Should go to his God in state,
With fifty file of Burmans
  To open him Heaven's Gate.

The men of the First Shikaris
  Marched till the break of day,
Till they came to the rebel village.
  The village of Pabengmay –
A *jingal* covered the clearing,
  Calthrops hampered the way.

Subadar Prag Tewarri,
  Bidding them load with ball,
Halted a dozen rifles
  Under the village wall;
Sent out a flanking-party
  With Jemadar Hira Lal.

The men of the First Shikaris
  Shouted and smote and slew,
Turning the grinning *jingal*
  On to the howling crew.
The Jemadar's flanking-party
  Butchered the folk who flew.

Long was the morn of slaughter,
  Long was the list of slain,
Five score heads were taken,
  Five score heads and twain;
And the men of the First Shikaris
  Went back to their grave again,

Each man bearing a basket
  Red as his palms that day,
Red as the blazing village –
  The village of Pabengmay.
And the '*drip-drip-drip*' from the baskets
  Reddened the grass by the way.

They made a pile of their trophies
　　High as a tall man's chin,
Head upon head distorted.
　　Set in a sightless grin,
Anger and pain and terror
　　Stamped on the smoke-scorched skin.

Subadar Prag Tewarri
　　Put the head of the Boh
On the top of the mound of triumph,
　　The head of his son below –
With the sword and the peacock-banner
　　That the world might behold and know.

Thus the *samadh* was perfect,
　　Thus was the lesson plain
Of the wrath of the First Shikaris –
　　The price of a white man slain;
And the men of the First Shikaris
　　Went back into camp again.

Then a silence came to the river,
　　A hush fell over the shore,
And Bohs that were brave departed,
　　And Sniders squibbed no more;
For the Burmans said
　　That a white man's head
Must be paid for with heads five-score.

There's a widow in sleepy Chester
　　Who weeps for her only son;
There's a grave on the Pabeng River,
　　A grave that the Burmans shun;
And there's Subadar Prag Tewarri
　　Who tells how the work was done.

L'Envoi to 'Departmental Ditties'

The smoke upon your Altar dies,
  The flowers decay,
The Goddess of your sacrifice
  Has flown away.
What profit then to sing or slay
The sacrifice from day to day?

'We know the Shrine is void,' they said,
  'The Goddess flown –
Yet wreaths are on the altar laid –
  The Altar-Stone
Is black with fumes of sacrifice,
Albeit She has fled our eyes.

'For, it may be, if still we sing
  And tend the Shrine,
Some Deity on wandering wing
  May there incline;
And, finding all in order meet,
Stay while we worship at Her feet.'

Dedication from 'Barrack-Room Ballads'

Beyond the path of the outmost sun through utter
      darkness hurled –
Farther than ever comet flared or vagrant stardust
      swirled –
Live such as fought and sailed and ruled and
      loved and made our world.

They are purged of pride because they died; they
      know the worth of their bays;
They sit at wine with the Maidens Nine and the
      Gods of the Elder Days –
It is their will to serve or be still as fitteth Our
      Father's praise.

'Tis theirs to sweep through the ringing deep
      where Azrael's outposts are,
Or buffet a path through the Pit's red wrath when
      God goes out to war,
Or hang with the reckless Seraphim on the rein of
      a red-maned star.

They take their mirth in the joy of the Earth –
      they dare not grieve for her pain.
They know of toil and the end of toil; they know
      God's Law is plain;
So they whistle the Devil to make them sport who
      know that Sin is vain.

And oft-times cometh our wise Lord God, master
      of every trade,
And tells them tales of His daily toil, of Edens
      newly made;

And they rise to their feet as He passes by,
    gentlemen unafraid.

To these who are cleansed of base Desire, Sorrow
    and Lust and Shame –
Gods for they knew the hearts of men, men for
    they stooped to Fame –
Borne on the breath that men call Death, my
    brother's spirit came.

He scarce had need to doff his pride or slough the
    dross of Earth –
E'en as he trod that day to God so walked he from
    his birth,
In simpleness and gentleness and honour and
    clean mirth.

So cup to lip in fellowship they gave him welcome
    high
And made him place at the banquet board – the
    Strong Men ranged thereby,
Who had done his work and held his peace and
    had no fear to die.

Beyond the loom of the last lone star, through
    open darkness hurled,
Further than rebel comet dared or hiving star-
    swarm swirled,
Sits he with those that praise our God for that
    they served His world.

Sestina of the Tramp-Royal

Speakin' in general, I 'ave tried 'em all –
The 'appy roads that take you o'er the world.
Speakin' in general, I 'ave found them good
For such as cannot use one bed too long,
But must get 'ence, the same as I 'ave done,
An' go observin' matters till they die.

What do it matter where or 'ow we die,
So long as we've our 'ealth to watch it all –
The different ways that different things are done.
An' men an' women lovin' in this world;
Takin' our chances as they come along,
An' when they ain't, pretendin' they are good?

In cash or credit – no, it aren't no good;
You 'ave to 'ave the 'abit or you'd die,
Unless you lived your life but one day long,
Nor didn't prophesy nor fret at all,
But drew your tucker some'ow from the world,
An' never bothered what you might ha' done.

But, Gawd, what things are they I 'aven't done?
I've turned my 'and to most, an' turned it good,
In various situations round the world –
For 'im that doth not work must surely die;
But that's no reason man should labour all
'Is life on one same shift – life's none so long.

Therefore, from job to job I've moved along.
Pay couldn't 'old me when my time was done,
For something in my 'ead upset it all,
Till I 'ad dropped whatever 'twas for good,

An', out at sea, be'eld the dock-lights die,
An' met my mate – the wind that tramps the world!

It's like a book, I think, this bloomin' world,
Which you can read and care for just so long,
But presently you feel that you will die
Unless you get the page you're readin' done,
An' turn another – likely not so good;
But what you're after is to turn 'em all.

Gawd bless this world! Whatever she 'ath done –
Excep' when awful long – I've found it good.
So write, before I die, "'E liked it all!"

1896

The Broken Men

For things we never mention,
  For Art misunderstood –
For excellent intention
  That did not turn to good;
From ancient tales' renewing,
  From clouds we would not clear –
Beyond the Law's pursuing
  We fled, and settled here.

We took no tearful leaving,
  We bade no long goodbyes.
Men talked of crime and thieving,
  Men wrote of fraud and lies.
To save our injured feelings
  'Twas time and time to go –
Behind was dock and Dartmoor,
  Ahead lay Callao!

The widow and the orphan
  That pray for ten per cent,
They clapped their trailers on us
  To spy the road we went.
They watched the foreign sailings
  (They scan the shipping still),
And that's your Christian people
  Returning good for ill!

God bless the thoughtful islands
  Where never warrants come;
God bless the just Republics
  That give a man a home,
That ask no foolish questions,

But set him on his feet;
And save his wife and daughters
    From the workhouse and the street!

On church and square and market
    The noonday silence falls:
You'll hear the drowsy mutter
    Of the fountain in our halls.
Asleep amid the yuccas
    The city takes her ease –
Till twilight brings the land-wind
    To the clicking jalousies.

Day long the diamond weather,
    The high, unaltered blue –
The smell of goats and incense
    And the mule-bells tinkling through.
Day long the warder ocean
    That keeps us from our kin,
And once a month our levée
    When the English mail comes in.

You'll find us up and waiting
    To treat you at the bar;
You'll find us less exclusive
    Than the average English are.
We'll meet you with a carriage,
    Too glad to show you round,
But – we do not lunch on steamers,
    For they are English ground.

We sail o' nights to England
    And join our smiling Boards –
Our wives go in with Viscounts

45

And our daughters dance with Lords,
But behind our princely doings,
    And behind each group we make,
We feel there's Something Waiting,
    And – we meet It when we wake.

Ah, God! One sniff of England –
    To greet our flesh and blood –
To hear the traffic slurring
    Once more through London mud!
Our towns of wasted honour –
    Our streets of lost delight!
How stands the old Lord Warden?
    Are Dover's cliffs still white?

1902

Gethsemane

The Garden called Gethsemane
    In Picardy it was,
And there the people came to see
    The English soldiers pass.
We used to pass – we used to pass
    Or halt, as it might be,
And ship our masks in case of gas
    Beyond Gethsemane.

The Garden called Gethsemane.
    It held a pretty lass,
But all the time she talked to me
    I prayed my cup might pass.
The officer sat on the chair,
    The men lay on the grass,
And all the time we halted there
    I prayed my cup might pass.

It didn't pass – it didn't pass –
    It didn't pass from me.
I drank it when we met the gas
    Beyond Gethsemane!

1914–18

The Pro-Consuls

Lord Milner

The overfaithful sword returns the user
His heart's desire at price of his heart's blood.
The clamour of the arrogant accuser
Wastes that one hour we needed to make good.
This was foretold of old at our outgoing;
This we accepted who have squandered, knowing,
The strength and glory of our reputations
At the day's need, as it were dross, to guard
The tender and new-dedicate foundations
Against the sea we fear – not man's award.

They that dig foundations deep,
    Fit for realms to rise upon,
Little honour do they reap
    Of their generation,
Any more than mountains gain
Stature till we reach the plain.

With no veil before their face
    Such as shroud or sceptre lend –
Daily in the marketplace,
Of one height to foe and friend –
    They must cheapen self to find
Ends uncheapened for mankind.

Through the night when hirelings rest,
    Sleepless they arise, alone,
The unsleeping arch to test
    And the o'er-trusted cornerstone,
'Gainst the need, they know, that lies
Hid behind the centuries.

Not by lust of praise or show,
   Not by Peace herself betrayed –
Peace herself must they forgo
   Till that peace be fitly made;
And in single strength uphold
Wearier hands and hearts acold.

On the stage their act hath framed
   For thy sports, O Liberty!
Doubted are they, and defamed
   By the tongues their act set free,
While they quicken, tend and raise
Power that must their power displace.

Lesser men feign greater goals,
   Failing whereof they may sit
Scholarly to judge the souls
   That go down into the Pit
And, despite its certain clay,
Heave a new world toward the day.

These at labour make no sign,
   More than planets, tides or years
Which discover God's design,
   Not our hopes and not our fears;
Nor in aught they gain or lose
Seek a triumph or excuse!

For, so the Ark be borne to Zion, who
Heeds how they perished or were paid that bore it
For, so the Shrine abide, what shame – what pride –
If we, the priests, were bound or crowned before it?

The Sea and the Hills

Who hath desired the Sea? – the sight of salt water
    unbounded –
The heave and the halt and the hurl and the crash
    of the comber wind-hounded?
The sleek-barrelled swell before storm, grey,
    foamless, enormous, and growing –
Stark calm on the lap of the Line or the crazy-
    eyed hurricane blowing –
His Sea in no showing the same – his Sea and the
    same 'neath each showing:
        His Sea as she slackens or thrills?
So and no otherwise – so and no otherwise –
    hillmen desire their Hills!

Who hath desired the Sea? – the immense and
    contemptuous surges?
The shudder, the stumble, the swerve, as the star-
    stabbing bowsprit emerges?
The orderly clouds of the Trades, the ridged,
    roaring sapphire thereunder –
Unheralded cliff-haunting flaws and the headsail's
    low-volleying thunder –
His Sea in no wonder the same – his Sea and the
    same through each wonder:
        His Sea as she rages or stills?
So and no otherwise – so and no otherwise –
    hillmen desire their Hills.

Who hath desired the Sea? Her menaces swift as
    her mercies?
The in-rolling walls of the fog and the silver-
    winged breeze that disperses?

The unstable mined berg going South and the
      calvings and groans that declare it –
White water half-guessed overside and the moon
      breaking timely to bare it –
His Sea as his fathers have dared – his Sea as his
      children shall dare it:
              His Sea as she serves him or kills?
So and no otherwise – so and no otherwise –
      hillmen desire their Hills.

Who hath desired the Sea? Her excellent loneliness
      rather
Than forecourts of kings, and her outermost pits
      than the streets where men gather
Inland, among dust, under trees – inland where
      the slayer may slay him –
Inland, out of reach of her arms, and the bosom
      whereon he must lay him –
His Sea from the first that betrayed – at the last
      that shall never betray him:
              His Sea that his being fulfils?
So and no otherwise – so and no otherwise –
      hillmen desire their Hills.

1902

McAndrew's Hymn

Lord, Thou hast made this world below the
      shadow of a dream,
An', taught by time, I tak' it so – exceptin' always
      Steam.
From coupler-flange to spindle-guide I see Thy
      Hand, O God –
Predestination in the stride o' yon connectin'-rod.
John Calvin might ha' forged the same –
      enorrmous, certain, slow –
Ay, wrought it in the furnace-flame – *my* 'Institutio'.
I cannot get my sleep tonight; old bones are hard
      to please;
I'll stand the middle watch up here – alone wi'
      God an' these
My engines, after ninety days o' race an' rack an'
      strain
Through all the seas of all Thy world, slam-
      bangin' home again.
Slam-bang too much – they knock a wee – the
      crosshead-gibs are loose,
But thirty thousand mile o' sea has gied them fair
      excuse . . .
Fine, clear an' dark – a full-draught breeze, wi'
      Ushant out o' sight,
An' Ferguson relievin' Hay. Old girl, ye'll walk
      tonight!
His wife's at Plymouth . . . Seventy – One – Two –
      Three since he began –
Three turns for Mistress Ferguson . . . and who's
      to blame the man?
There's none at any port for me, by drivin' fast or
      slow,

Since Elsie Campbell went to Thee, Lord, thirty
    years ago.
(The year the *Sarah Sands* was burned. Oh, roads
    we used to tread,
Fra' Maryhill to Pollokshaws – fra' Govan to
    Parkhead!)
Not but they're ceevil on the Board. Ye'll hear Sir
    Kenneth say:
'Good morrn, McAndrew! Back again? An' how's
    your bilge today?'
Miscallin' technicalities but handin' me my chair
To drink Madeira wi' three Earls – the auld Fleet
    Engineer
That started as a boiler-whelp – when steam and
    he were low.
I mind the time we used to serve a broken pipe wi'
    tow!
Ten pound was all the pressure then – Eh! Eh! – a
    man wad drive;
An' here, our workin' gauges give one hunder
    sixty-five!
We're creepin' on wi' each new rig – less weight
    an' larger power;
There'll be the loco-boiler next an' thirty mile an'
    hour!
Thirty an' more. What I ha' seen since ocean-
    steam began
Leaves me na doot for the machine: but what
    about the man?
The man that counts, wi' all his runs, one million
    mile o' sea:
Four time the span from earth to moon . . . How
    far, O Lord, from Thee

That wast beside him night an' day? Ye mind my
    first typhoon?
It scoughed the skipper on his way to jock wi' the
    saloon.
Three feet were on the stokehold-floor – just
    slappin' to an' fro –
An' cast me on a furnace-door. I have the marks
    to show.
Marks! I ha' marks o' more than burns – deep in
    my soul an' black,
An' times like this, when things go smooth, my
    wickudness comes back.
The sins o' four an' forty years, all up an' down
    the seas,
Clack an' repeat like valves half-fed . . . Forgie's
    our trespasses!
Nights when I'd come on deck to mark, wi' envy
    in my gaze,
The couples kittlin' in the dark between the
    funnel-stays;
Years when I raked the Ports wi' pride to fill my
    cup o' wrong –
Judge not, O Lord, my steps aside at Gay Street
    in Hong-Kong!
Blot out the wastrel hours of mine in sin when I
    abode –
Jane Harrigan's an' Number Nine, The Reddick
    an' Grant Road!
An' waur than all – my crownin' sin – rank
    blasphemy an' wild.
I was not four and twenty then – Ye wadna judge
    a child?
I'd seen the Tropics first that run – new fruit, new
    smells, new air –

How could I tell – blind-fou wi' sun – the Deil
    was lurkin' there?
By day like playhouse-scenes the shore slid past
    our sleepy eyes;
By night those soft, lasceevious stars leered from
    those velvet skies,
In port (we used no cargo-steam) I'd daunder
    down the streets –
An ijjit grinnin' in a dream – for shells an' parrakeets,
An' walkin'-sticks o' carved bamboo an' blowfish
    stuffed an' dried –
Fillin' my bunk wi' rubbishry the Chief put overside.
Till, off Sambawa Head, Ye mind, I heard a land-
    breeze ca',
Milk-warm wi' breath o' spice an' bloom:
    'McAndrew, come awa'!'
Firm, clear an' low – no haste, no hate – the
    ghostly whisper went,
Just statin' eevidential facts beyon' all argument:
'Your mither's God's a graspin' deil, the shadow
    o' yoursel',
Got out o' books by meenisters clean daft on
    Heaven an' Hell.
They mak' him in the Broomielaw, o' Glasgie cold
    an' dirt,
A jealous, pridefu' fetich, lad, that's only strong to
    hurt.
Ye'll not go back to Him again an' kiss His red-
    hot rod,
But come wi' Us' (Now, who were *They?*) 'an'
    know the Leevin' God,
That does not kipper souls for sport or break a life
    in jest,

But swells the ripenin' cocoanuts an' ripes the
    woman's breast.'
An' there it stopped – cut off – no more – that
    quiet, certain voice –
For me, six months o' twenty-four, to leave or
    take at choice.
'Twas on me like a thunderclap – it racked me
    through an' through –
Temptation past the show o' speech, unnameable
    an' new –
The Sin against the Holy Ghost? . . . An' under
    all, our screw.

That storm blew by but left behind her anchor-
    shiftin' swell.
Thou knowest all my heart an' mind, Thou
    knowest, Lord, I fell –
Third on the *Mary Gloster* then, and first that
    night in Hell!
Yet was Thy Hand beneath my head, about my
    feet Thy Care –
Fra' Deli clear to Torres Strait, the trial o' despair,
But when we touched the Barrier Reef Thy
    answer to my prayer! . . .
We dared na run that sea by night but lay an' held
    our fire,
An' I was drowsin' on the hatch – sick – sick wi'
    doubt an' tire:
'*Better the sight of eyes that see than wanderin' o'
    desire!*'
Ye mind that word? Clear as our gongs – again,
    an' once again,
When rippin' down through coral-trash ran out
    our moorin'-chain:

An', by Thy Grace, I had the Light to see my duty
  plain.
Light on the engine-room – no more – bright as
  our carbons burn.
I've lost it since a thousand times, but never past
  return!

*   *   *

Obsairve! Per annum we'll have here two thousand
  souls aboard –
Think not I dare to justify myself before the Lord,
But – average fifteen hunder souls safe-borne fra'
  port to port –
I *am* o' service to my kind. Ye wadna blame the
  thought?
Maybe they steam from Grace to Wrath – to sin
  by folly led –
It isna mine to judge their path – their lives are on
  my head.
Mine at the last – when all is done it all comes
  back to me,
The fault that leaves six thousand ton a log upon
  the sea.
We'll tak' one stretch – three weeks an' odd by
  ony road ye steer –
Fra' Cape Town east to Wellington – ye need an
  engineer.
Fail there – ye've time to weld your shaft – ay, eat
  it, ere ye're spoke;
Or make Kerguelen under sail – three jiggers
  burned wi' smoke!
An' home again – the Rio run: it's no child's play
  to go

57

Steamin' to bell for fourteen days o' snow an' floe
an' blow.
The bergs like kelpies overside that girn an' turn
an' shift
Whaur, grindin' like the Mills o'God, goes by the
big South drift.
(Hail, Snow and Ice that praise the Lord. I've met
them at their work,
An' wished we had anither route or they anither
kirk.)
Yon's strain, hard strain, o' head an' hand, for
though Thy Power brings
All skill to naught, Ye'll understand a man must
think o' things.
Then, at the last, we'll get to port an' hoist their
baggage clear –
The passengers, wi' gloves an' canes – an' this is
what I'll hear:
'Well, thank ye for a pleasant voyage. The
tender's comin' now.'
While I go testin' follower-bolts an' watch the
skipper bow.
They've words for every one but me – shake
hands wi' half the crew,
Except the dour Scots engineer, the man they
never knew.
An' yet I like the wark for all we've dam'-few
pickin's here –
No pension, an' the most we'll earn's four hunder
pound a year.
Better myself abroad? Maybe. *I'd* sooner starve
than sail
Wi' such as call a snifter-rod *ross* . . . French for
nightingale.

Commeesion on my stores? Some do; but I
    cannot afford
To lie like stewards wi' patty-pans. I'm older than
    the Board.
A bonus on the coal I save? Ou ay, the Scots are
    close,
But when I grudge the strength Ye gave I'll
    grudge their food to *those*.
(There's bricks that I might recommend – an'
    clink the firebars cruel.
No! Welsh – Wangarti at the worst – an' damn all
    patent fuel!)
Inventions? Ye must stay in port to mak' a patent
    pay.
My Deeferential Valve-Gear taught me how that
    business lay.
I blame no chaps wi' clearer heads for aught they
    make or sell.
I found that I could not invent an' look to these as
    well.
So, wrestled wi' Apollyon – Nah! – fretted like a
    bairn –
But burned the workin'-plans last run, wi' all I
    hoped to earn.
Ye know how hard an Idol dies, an' what that
    meant to me –
E'en tak' it for a sacrifice acceptable to Thee . . .
*Below there! Oiler! What's your wark? Ye find it
    runnin' hard?*
Ye needn't swill the cup wi' oil – this isn't the Cunard!
*Ye thought? Ye are not paid to think. Go, sweat that
    off again!*
Tck! Tck! It's deeficult to sweer nor tak' The
    Name in vain!

Men, ay, an' women, call me stern. Wi' these to
    oversee,
Ye'll note I've little time to burn on social repartee.
The bairns see what their elders miss; they'll hunt
    me to an' fro,
Till for the sake of – well, a kiss – I tak' 'em down
    below.
That minds me of our Viscount loon – Sir Kenneth's
    kin – the chap
Wi' Russia-leather tennis-shoon an' spar-decked
    yachtin'cap.
I showed him round last week, o'er all – an' at the
    last says he:
'Mister McAndrew, don't you think steam spoils
    romance at sea?'
Damned iijit! I'd been doon that morn to see what
    ailed the throws,
Manholin', on my back – the cranks three inches
    off my nose.
Romance! Those first-class passengers they like it
    very well,
Printed an' bound in little books; but why don't
    poets tell?
I'm sick of all their quirks an' turns – the loves an'
    doves they dream –
Lord, send a man like Robbie Burns to sing the
    Song o' Steam!
To match wi' Scotia's noblest speech yon orchestra
    sublime
Whaurto – uplifted like the Just – the tail-rods
    mark the time.
The crank-throws give the double-bass, the feed-
    pump sobs an' heaves,

An' now the main eccentrics start their quarrel on
the sheaves:
Her time, her own appointed time, the rocking
link-head bides,
Till – hear that note? – the rod's return whings
glimmerin' through the guides.
They're all awa'! True beat, full power, the
clangin' chorus goes
Clear to the tunnel where they sit, my purrin'
dynamoes.
Interdependence absolute, foreseen, ordained,
decreed,
To work, Ye'll note, at ony tilt an' every rate o'
speed.
Fra' skylight-lift to furnace-bars, backed, bolted,
braced an' stayed,
An' singin' like the Mornin' Stars for joy that they
are made;
While, out o' touch o' vanity, the sweatin' thrust-
block says:
'Not unto us the praise, or man – not unto us the
praise!'
Now, a' together, hear them lift their lesson –
theirs an' mine:
'Law, Orrder, Duty an' Restraint, Obedience,
Discipline!'
Mill, forge an' try-pit taught them that when
roarin' they arose,
An' whiles I wonder if a soul was gied them wi'
the blows.
Oh for a man to weld it then, in one trip-hammer
strain,
Till even first-class passengers could tell the
meanin' plain!

But no one cares except mysel' that serve an'
    understand
My seven thousand horsepower here. Eh, Lord!
    They're grand – they're grand!
Uplift am I? When first in store the new-made
    beasties stood,
Were Ye cast down that breathed the Word
    declarin' all things good?
Not so! O' that warld-liftin' joy no after-fall could
    vex,
Ye've left a glimmer still to cheer the Man – the
    Arrtifex!
That holds, in spite o' knock and scale, o' friction,
    waste an' slip,
An' by that light – now, mark my word – we'll
    build the Perfect Ship.
I'll never last to judge her lines or take her curve –
    not I.
But I ha' lived an' I ha' worked. Be thanks to
    Thee, Most High!
An' I ha' done what I ha' done – judge Thou if ill
    or well –
Always Thy Grace preventin' me . . .
               Losh! Yon's the 'Stand-by' bell.
Pilot so soon? His flare it is. The mornin'-watch is
    set.
Well, God be thanked, as I was sayin', I'm no
    Pelagian yet.
Now I'll tak' on . . .
    'Morrn, Ferguson. Man, have ye ever thought
What your good leddy costs in coal? . . . I'll burn 'em
    down to port.

1893

62

The 'Mary Gloster'

I've paid for your sickest fancies; I've humoured
    your crackedest whim –
Dick, it's your daddy, dying; you've got to listen
    to him!
Good for a fortnight, am I? The doctor told you?
    He lied.
I shall go under by morning, and – Put that nurse
    outside.
'Never seen death yet, Dickie? Well, now is your
    time to learn,
And you'll wish you held my record before it
    comes to your turn.
Not counting the Line and the Foundry, the
    Yards and the village, too,
I've made myself and a million; but I'm damned if
    I made you.
Master at two-and-twenty, and married at twenty-
    three –
Ten thousand men on the payroll, and forty
    freighters at sea!
Fifty years between 'em, and every year of it fight,
And now I'm Sir Anthony Gloster, dying, a
    baronite:
For I lunched with his Royal 'Ighness – what was
    it the papers had?
'Not least of our merchant-princes.' Dickie, that's
    me, your dad!
I didn't begin with askings. *I* took my job and I
    stuck;
I took the chances they wouldn't, an' now they're
    calling it luck.

Lord, what boats I've handled – rotten and leaky
    and old –
Ran 'em, or – opened the bilge-cock, precisely as I
    was told.
Grub that 'ud bind you crazy, and crews that 'ud
    turn you grey,
And a big fat lump of insurance to cover the risk
    on the way.
The others they dursn't do it; they said they
    valued their life
(They've served me since as skippers). *I* went, and
    I took my wife.
Over the world I drove 'em, married at twenty-
    three,
And your mother saving the money and making a
    man of me.
I was content to be master, but she said there was
    better behind;
She took the chances I wouldn't, and I followed
    your mother blind.
She egged me to borrow the money, an' she
    helped me to clear the loan,
When we bought half-shares in a cheap 'un and
    hoisted a flag of our own.
Patching and coaling on credit, and living the
    Lord knew how,
We started the Red Ox freighters – we've eight-
    and-thirty now.
And those were the days of clippers, and the
    freights were clipper-freights,
And we knew we were making our fortune, but
    she died in Macassar Straits –
By the Little Paternosters, as you come to the
    Union Bank –

64

And we dropped her in fourteen fathom: I pricked
    it off where she sank.
Owners we were, full owners, and the boat was
    christened for her,
And she died in the *Mary Gloster*. My heart, how
    young we were!
So I went on a spree round Java and well-nigh ran
    her ashore,
But your mother came and warned me and I
    wouldn't liquor no more:
Strict I stuck to my business, afraid to stop or I'd
    think,
Saving the money (she warned me), and letting
    the other men drink.
And I met M'Cullough in London (I'd saved five
    'undred then),
And 'tween us we started the Foundry – three
    forges and twenty men.
Cheap repairs for the cheap 'uns. It paid, and the
    business grew;
For I bought me a steam-lathe patent, and that
    was a gold mine too.
'Cheaper to build 'em than buy 'em,' *I* said, but
    M'Cullough he shied,
And we wasted a year in talking before we moved
    to the Clyde.
And the Lines were all beginning, and we all of us
    started fair,
Building our engines like houses and staying the
    boilers square.
But M'Cullough 'e wanted cabins with marble
    and maple and all,
And Brussels an' Utrecht velvet, and baths and a
    Social Hall,

And pipes for closets all over, and cutting the
    frames too light,
But M'Cullough he died in the Sixties, and – Well,
    I'm dying tonight . . .
I knew – *I* knew what was coming, when we bid
    on the *Byfleet's* keel –
They piddled and piffled with iron. I'd given my
    orders for steel!
Steel and the first expansions. It paid, I tell you, it
    paid,
When we came with our nine-knot freighters and
    collared the long-run trade!
And they asked me how I did it, and I gave 'em
    the Scripture text,
'You keep your light so shining a little in front o'
    the next!'
They copied all they could follow, but they
    couldn't copy my mind,
And I left 'em sweating and stealing a year and a
    half behind.
Then came the armour-contracts, but that was
    M'Cullough's side;
He was always best in the Foundry, but better,
    perhaps, he died.
I went through his private papers; the notes was
    plainer than print;
And I'm no fool to finish if a man'll give me a
    hint.
(I remember his widow was angry.) So I saw what
    his drawings meant,
And I started the six-inch rollers, and it paid me
    sixty per cent.
Sixty per cent *with* failures, and more than twice
    we could do,

And a quarter-million to credit, and I saved it all
     for you!
I thought – it doesn't matter – you seemed to
     favour your ma,
But you're nearer forty than thirty, and I know the
     kind you are.
Harrer an' Trinity College! I ought to ha' sent you
     to sea –
But I stood you an education, an' what have you
     done for me?
The things I knew was proper you wouldn't thank
     me to give,
And the things I knew was rotten you said was the
     way to live.
For you muddled with books and pictures, an'
     china an' etchin's an' fans,
And your rooms at college was beastly – more like
     a whore's than a man's;
Till you married that thin-flanked woman, as
     white and as stale as a bone,
An' she gave you your social nonsense; but
     where's that kid o' your own?
I've seen your carriages blocking the half o' the
     Cromwell Road,
But never the doctor's brougham to help the
     missus unload.
(So there isn't even a grandchild, an' the Gloster
     family's done.)
Not like your mother, she isn't. *She* carried her
     freight each run.
But they died, the pore little beggars! At sea she
     had 'em – they died.
Only you, an' you stood it. You haven't stood
     much beside.

Weak, a liar, and idle, and mean as a collier's
    whelp
Nosing for scraps in the galley. No help – my son
    was no help!
So he gets three 'undred thousand, in trust and
    the interest paid.
I wouldn't give it you, Dickie – you see, I made it
    in trade.
You're saved from soiling your fingers, and if you
    have no child,
It all comes back to the business. 'Gad, won't
    your wife be wild!
Calls and calls in her carriage, her 'andkerchief up
    to 'er eye:
Daddy! dear daddy's dyin'!' and doing her best to
    cry.
Grateful? Oh, yes, I'm grateful, but keep her away
    from here.
Your mother 'ud never ha' stood 'er, and, anyhow,
    women are queer . . .
There's women will say I've married a second
    time. Not quite!
But give pore Aggie a hundred, and tell her your
    lawyers'll fight.
She was the best o' the boiling – you'll meet her
    before it ends.
I'm in for a row with the mother – I'll leave you
    settle my friends.
For a man he must go with a woman, which
    women don't understand –
Or the sort that say they can see it they aren't the
    marrying brand.
But I wanted to speak o' your mother that's Lady
    Gloster still;

I'm going to up and see her, without its hurting
the will.
Here! Take your hand off the bell-pull. Five
thousand's waiting for you,
If you'll only listen a minute, and do as I bid you
do.
They'll try to prove me crazy, and, if you bungle,
they can;
And I've only you to trust to! (O God, why ain't it
a man?)
There's some waste money on marbles, the same
as M'Cullough tried –
Marbles and mausoleums – but I call that sinful
pride.
There's some ship bodies for burial – we've
carried 'em, soldered and packed;
Down in their wills they wrote it, and nobody
called *them* cracked.
But me – I've too much money, and people might
. . . All my fault:
It come o' hoping for grandsons and buying that
Wokin' vault . . .
I'm sick o' the 'ole dam' business. I'm going back
where I came.
Dick, you're the son o' my body, and you'll take
charge o' the same!
I want to lie by your mother, ten thousand mile
away,
And they'll want to send me to Woking; and that's
where you'll earn your pay.
I've thought it out on the quiet, the same as it
ought to be done –
Quiet, and decent, and proper – an' here's your
orders, my son.

You know the Line? You don't, though. You write
    to the Board, and tell
Your father's death has upset you an' you're goin'
    to cruise for a spell,
An' you'd like the *Mary Gloster* – I've held her
    ready for this –
They'll put her in working order and you'll take
    her out as she is.
Yes, it was money idle when I patched her and
    laid her aside
(Thank God, I can pay for my fancies!) – the boat
    where your mother died,
By the Little Paternosters, as you come to the
    Union Bank,
We dropped her – I think I told you – and I
    pricked it off where she sank.
['Tiny she looked on the grating – that oily,
    treacly sea –]
'Hundred and Eighteen East, remember, and
    South just Three.
Easy bearings to carry – Three South – Three to
    the dot;
But I gave McAndrew a copy in case of dying – or
    not.
And so you'll write to McAndrew, he's Chief of
    the Maori Line;
They'll give him leave, if you ask 'em and say it's
    business o' mine.
I built three boats for the Maoris, an' very well
    pleased they were,
An' I've known Mac since the Fifties, and Mac
    knew me – and her.
After the first stroke warned me I sent him the
    money to keep

Against the time you'd claim it, committin' your
      dad to the deep;
For you are the son o' my body, and Mac was my
      oldest friend,
I've never asked 'im to dinner, but he'll see it out
      to the end.
Stiff-necked Glasgow beggar! I've heard he's
      prayed for my soul,
But he couldn't lie if you paid him, and he'd
      starve before he stole.
He'll take the *Mary* in ballast – you'll find her a
      lively ship;
And you'll take Sir Anthony Gloster, that goes on
      'is wedding-trip,
Lashed in our old deck-cabin with all three
      portholes wide,
The kick o' the screw beneath him and the round
      blue seas outside!
Sir Anthony Gloster's carriage – our 'ouse-flag
      flyin' free –
Ten thousand men on the payroll and forty
      freighters at sea!
He made himself and a million, but this world is a
      fleetin' show,
And he'll go to the wife of 'is bosom the same as
      he ought to go –
By the heel of the Paternosters – there isn't a
      chance to mistake –
And Mac'll pay you the money as soon as the
      bubbles break!
Five thousand for six weeks' cruising, the staunchest
      freighter afloat,
And Mac he'll give you your bonus the minute
      I'm out o' the boat!

He'll take you round to Macassar, and you'll
    come back alone;
He knows what I want o' the *Mary* . . . I'll do
    what I please with my own.
Your mother 'ud call it wasteful, but I've seven-
    and-thirty more;
I'll come in my private carriage and bid it wait at
    the door . . .
For my son 'e was never a credit: 'e muddled with
    books and art,
And 'e lived on Sir Anthony's money and 'e broke
    Sir Anthony's heart.
There isn't even a grandchild, and the Gloster
    family's done –
The only one you left me – O mother, the only
    one!
Harrer and Trinity College – me slavin' early an'
    late –
An' he thinks I'm dying crazy, and you're in
    Macassar Strait!
Flesh o' my flesh, my dearie, for ever an' ever
    amen,
That first stroke come for a warning. I ought to
    ha' gone to you then.
But – cheap repairs for a cheap 'un – the doctors
    said I'd do.
Mary, why didn't *you* warn me? I've allus heeded
    to you,
Excep' – I know – about women; but you are a
    spirit now;
An', wife, they was only women, and I was a man.
    That's how.
An' a man 'e must go with a woman, as you *could*
    not understand;

But I never talked 'em secrets. I paid 'em out o'
    hand.
Thank Gawd, I can pay for my fancies! Now
    what's five thousand to me,
For a berth off the Paternosters in the haven
    where I would be?
I believe in the Resurrection, if I read my Bible
    plain,
But I wouldn't trust 'em at Wokin'; we're safer at
    sea again.
For the heart it shall go with the treasure – go
    down to the sea in ships.
I'm sick of the hired women. I'll kiss my girl on
    her lips!
I'll be content with my fountain. I'll drink from
    my own well,
And the wife of my youth shall charm me – an'
    the rest can go to Hell!
(Dickie, *he* will, that's certain.) I'll lie in our
    standin'-bed,
An' Mac'll take her in ballast – an' she trims best
    by the head . . .
Down by the head an' sinkin', her fires are drawn
    and cold,
And the water's splashin' hollow on the skin of
    the empty hold –
Churning an' choking and chuckling, quiet and
    scummy and dark –
Full to her lower hatches and risin' steady. Hark!
That was the after-bulkhead . . . She's flooded
    from stem to stern . . .
'Never seen death yet, Dickie? . . . Well, now is
    your time to learn!

1894

The Ballad of the 'Bolivar'

Seven men from all the world back to Docks again,
Rolling down the Ratcliffe Road drunk and raising Cain.
Give the girls another drink 'fore we sign away –
We that took the 'Bolivar' out across the Bay!

We put out from Sunderland loaded down with
    rails;
    We put back to Sunderland 'cause our cargo
      shifted;
We put out from Sunderland – met the winter
    gales –
    Seven days and seven nights to The Start we
      drifted.

      Racketing her rivets loose, smokestack white
        as snow,
      All the coals adrift adeck, half the rails below,
      Leaking like a lobster-pot, steering like a dray –
      Out we took the *Bolivar*, out across the Bay!

One by one the Lights came up, winked and let us
    by;
    Mile by mile we waddled on, coal and fo'c'sle
      short;
Met a blow that laid us down, heard a bulkhead
    fly;
    Left The Wolf behind us with a two-foot list to
      port.

Trailing like a wounded duck, working out
    her soul;
Clanging like a smithy-shop after every roll;
Just a funnel and a mast lurching through the
    spray –
So we threshed the *Bolivar* out across the Bay!

Felt her hog and felt her sag, betted when she'd
    break;
  Wondered every time she raced if she'd stand
    the shock;
Heard the seas like drunken men pounding at her
    strake;
  Hoped the Lord 'ud keep His thumb on the
    plummer-block!

    Banged against the iron decks, bilges choked
      with coal;
    Flayed and frozen foot and hand, sick of
      heart and soul;
    'Last we prayed she'd buck herself into
      Judgment Day –
    Hi! we cursed the *Bolivar* knocking round the
      Bay!

O her nose flung up to sky, groaning to be still –
  Up and down and back we went, never time for
    breath;
Then the money paid at Lloyds' caught her by the
    keel,
  And the stars ran round and round dancin' at
    our death!

Aching for an hour's sleep, dozing off between:
  'Heard the rotten rivets draw when she took
    it green;
  'Watched the compass chase its tail like a cat
    at play –
  That was on the *Bolivar*, south across the Bay!

Once we saw between the squalls, lyin' head to
    swell –
  Mad with work and weariness, wishin' they was
    we –
Some damned liner's lights go by like a grand
    hotel;
  'Cheered her from the *Bolivar* swampin' in the sea.

    Then a greybeard cleared us out, then the
      skipper laughed;
    'Boys, the wheel has gone to Hell – rig the
      winches aft!
    Yoke the kicking rudder-head – get her under
      way!'
    So we steered her, pully-haul, out across the
      Bay!

Just a pack o' rotten plates puttied up with tar,
In we came, an' time enough, 'cross Bilbao Bar.
Overloaded, undermanned, meant to founder, we
Euchred God Almighty's storm, bluffed the Eternal
    Sea!

Seven men from all the world back to town again,
Rollin' down the Ratcliffe Road drunk and raising Cain:
Seven men from out of Hell. Ain't the owners gay,
Cause we took the 'Bolivar' safe across the Bay?

1890

The Destroyers

The strength of twice three thousand horse
That seeks the single goal;
The line that holds the rending course,
The hate that swings the whole:
The stripped hulls, slinking through the gloom,
At gaze and gone again –
The Brides of Death that wait the groom –
The Choosers of the Slain!

Offshore where sea and skyline blend
    In rain, the daylight dies;
The sullen, shouldering swells attend
    Night and our sacrifice.
Adown the stricken capes no flare –
    No mark on spit or bar, –
Girdled and desperate we dare
    The blindfold game of war.

Nearer the up-flung beams that spell
    The council of our foes;
Clearer the barking guns that tell
    Their scattered flank to close.
Sheer to the trap they crowd their way
    From ports for this unbarred.
Quiet, and count our laden prey,
    The convoy and her guard!

On shoal with scarce a foot below,
    Where rock and islet throng,
Hidden and hushed we watch them throw
    Their anxious lights along.

Not here, not here your danger lies –
   (Stare hard, O hooded eyne!)
Save where the dazed rock-pigeons rise
   The lit cliffs give no sign.

Therefore – to break the rest ye seek,
   The Narrow Seas to clear –
Hark to the siren's whimpering shriek –
   The driven death is here!
Look to your van a league away, –
   What midnight terror stays
The bulk that checks against the spray
   Her crackling tops ablaze?

Hit, and hard hit! The blow went home,
   The muffled, knocking stroke –
The steam that overruns the foam –
   The foam that thins to smoke –
The smoke that clokes the deep aboil –
   The deep that chokes her throes
Till, streaked with ash and sleeked with oil,
   The lukewarm whirlpools close!

A shadow down the sickened wave
   Long since her slayer fled:
But hear their chattering quick-fires rave
   Astern, abeam, ahead!
Panic that shells the drifting spar –
   Loud waste with none to check –
Mad fear that rakes a scornful star
   Or sweeps a consort's deck.

Now, while their silly smoke hangs thick,
   Now ere their wits they find,

Lay in and lance them to the quick –
   Our gallied whales are blind!
Good luck to those that see the end,
   Goodbye to those that drown –
For each his chance as chance shall send –
   And God for all! *Shut down!*

The strength of twice three thousand horse
   That serve the one command;
The hand that heaves the headlong force,
   The hate that backs the hand:
The doom-bolt in the darkness freed,
   The mine that splits the main;
The white-hot wake, the 'wildering speed –
   The Choosers of the Slain!

1898

A Song in Storm

Be well assured that on our side
    The abiding oceans fight,
Though headlong wind and heaping tide
    Make us their sport tonight.
By force of weather, not of war,
    In jeopardy we steer:
Then welcome Fate's discourtesy
    Whereby it shall appear
        How in all time of our distress,
        And our deliverance too,
            The game is more than the player of the
                game,
            And the ship is more than the crew!

Out of the mist into the mirk
    The glimmering combers roll.
Almost these mindless waters work
    As though they had a soul –
Almost as though they leagued to whelm
    Our flag beneath their green:
Then welcome Fate's discourtesy
    Whereby it shall be seen, etc.

Be well assured, though wave and wind
    Have mightier blows in store,
That we who keep the watch assigned
    Must stand to it the more;
And as our streaming bows rebuke
    Each billow's baulked career,
Sing, welcome Fate's discourtesy
    Whereby it is made clear, etc.

No matter though our decks be swept
    And mast and timber crack –
We can make good all loss except
    The loss of turning back.
So, 'twixt these Devils and our deep
    Let courteous trumpets sound,
To welcome Fate's discourtesy
    Whereby it will be found, etc.

Be well assured, though in our power
    Is nothing left to give
But chance and place to meet the hour,
    And leave to strive to live,
Till these dissolve our Order holds,
    Our Service binds us here.
Then welcome Fate's discourtesy
    Whereby it is made clear
        How in all time of our distress,
        As in our triumph too,
        The game is more than the player of the
            game,
        And the ship is more than the crew!

1914–18

The Long Trail

There's a whisper down the field where the year
    has shot her yield,
  And the ricks stand grey to the sun,
Singing: 'Over then, come over, for the bee has
    quit the clover,
  'And your English summer's done.'

    You have heard the beat of the offshore wind,
      And the thresh of the deep-sea rain;
    You have heard the song – how long? how long?
    Pull out on the trail again!
Ha' done with the Tents of Shem, dear lass,
We've seen the seasons through,
  And it's time to turn on the old trail, our own
    trail, the out trail,
  Pull out, pull out, on the Long Trail – the trail
    that is always new!

It's North you may run to the rime-ringed sun
  Or South to the blind Horn's hate;
Or East all the way into Mississippi Bay,
    Or West to the Golden Gate –
    Where the blindest bluffs hold good, dear lass,
      And the wildest tales are true,
    And the men bulk big on the old trail, our
      own trail, the out trail,
    And life runs large on the Long Trail – the
    trail that is always new.

The days are sick and cold, and the skies are grey
    and old,
  And the twice-breathed airs blow damp;

And I'd sell my tired soul for the bucking beam-
    sea roll
  Of a black Bilbao tramp,
    With her load-line over her hatch, dear lass,
    And a drunken Dago crew,
    And her nose held down on the old trail, our
      own trail, the out trail
    From Cadiz south on the Long Trail – the
    trail that is always new.

There be triple ways to take, of the eagle or the
    snake,
  Or the way of a man with a maid;
But the sweetest way to me is a ship's upon the
    sea
  In the heel of the North-East Trade.
    Can you hear the crash on her bows, dear lass,
    And the drum of the racing screw,
    As she ships it green on the old trail, our own
      trail, the out trail,
    As she lifts and 'scends on the Long Trail –
    the trail that is always new?

See the shaking funnels roar, with the Peter at the
    fore,
  And the fenders grind and heave,
And the derricks clack and grate, as the tackle
  hooks the crate,
  And the fall-rope whines through the sheave;
    It's 'Gangplank up and in,' dear lass,
    It's 'Hawsers warp her through!'
    And it's 'All clear aft' on the old trail, our
      own trail, the out trail,
    We're backing down on the Long Trail – the
    trail that is always new.

O the mutter overside, when the port-fog holds us
    tied,
  And the sirens hoot their dread,
When foot by foot we creep o'er the hueless,
    viewless deep
    To the sob of the questing lead!
      It's down by the Lower Hope, dear lass,
      With the Gunfleet Sands in view,
      Till the Mouse swings green on the old trail,
        our own trail, the out trail,
      And the Gull Light lifts on the Long Trail –
      the trail that is always new.

O the blazing tropic night, when the wake's a welt
    of light
  That holds the hot sky tame,
And the steady forefoot snores through the planet-
    powdered floors
    Where the scared whale flukes in flame!
      Her plates are flaked by the sun, dear lass,
      And her ropes are taut with the dew,
      For we're booming down on the old trail, our
        own trail, the out trail,
      We're sagging south on the Long Trail – the
      trail that is always new.

Then home, get her home, where the drunken
    rollers comb,
  And the shouting seas drive by,
And the engines stamp and ring, and the wet
    bows reel and swing,
    And the Southern Cross rides high!
      Yes, the old lost stars wheel back, dear lass,
      That blaze in the velvet blue.

They're all old friends on the old trail, our
    own trail, the out trail,
They're God's own guides on the Long Trail
    – the trail that is always new.

Fly forward, O my heart, from the Foreland to the
    Start –
    We're steaming all too slow,
And it's twenty thousand mile to our little lazy isle
    Where the trumpet-orchids blow!
        You have heard the call of the offshore wind
        And the voice of the deep-sea rain;
        You have heard the song – how long? – how
          long?
        Pull out on the trail again!

The Lord knows what we may find, dear lass,
And The Deuce knows what we may do –
But we're back once more on the old trail, our
    own trail, the out trail,
We're down, hull-down, on the Long Trail – the
    trail that is always new!

Ave Imperatrix!

*Written on the occasion of the attempt to
assassinate Queen Victoria in March 1882*

From every quarter of your land
   They give God thanks who turned away
Death and the needy madman's hand,
   Death-fraught, which menaced you that day.

One school of many made to make
   Men who shall hold it dearest right
To battle for their ruler's sake,
   And stake their being in the fight,

Sends greeting humble and sincere –
   Though verse be rude and poor and mean –
To you, the greatest as most dear –
   Victoria, by God's grace Our Queen!

Such greeting as should come from those
   Whose fathers faced the Sepoy hordes,
Or served you in the Russian snows,
   And, dying, left their sons their swords.

And some of us have fought for you
   Already in the Afghan pass –
Or where the scarce-seen smoke-puffs flew
   From Boer marksmen in the grass;

And all are bred to do your will
   By land and sea – wherever flies
The Flag, to fight and follow still,
   And work your Empire's destinies.

Once more we greet you, though unseen
   Our greeting be, and coming slow.
Trust us, if need arise, O Queen,
   We shall not tarry with the blow!

A Song of the English

Fair is our lot – O goodly is our heritage!
(Humble ye, my people, and be fearful in your mirth!)
  For the Lord our God Most High
  He hath made the deep as dry,
He hath smote for us a pathway to the ends of all the
    Earth!

Yea, though we sinned, and our rulers went from
    righteousness –
Deep in all dishonour though we stained our garments'
    hem,
  Oh, be ye not dismayed,
  Though we stumbled and we strayed,
We were led by evil counsellors – the Lord shall deal
    with them!

Hold ye the Faith – the Faith our Fathers sealed us;
Whoring not with visions – overwise and overstale.
  Except ye pay the Lord
  Single heart and single sword,
Of your children in their bondage He shall ask them
    treble-tale!

Keep ye the Law – be swift in all obedience –
Clear the land of evil, drive the road and bridge the
    ford.
  Make ye sure to each his own
  That he reap where he hath sown;
By the peace among Our peoples let men know we
    serve the Lord!

Hear now a song – a song of broken interludes –
A song of little cunning; of a singer nothing worth.
   Through the naked words and mean
   May ye see the truth between,
As the singer knew and touched it in the ends of all the
   Earth!

THE COASTWISE LIGHTS

Our brows are bound with spindrift and the weed
   is on our knees;
Our loins are battered 'neath us by the swinging,
   smoking seas.
From reef and rock and skerry – over headland,
   ness, and voe –
The Coastwise Lights of England watch the ships
   of England go!

Through the endless summer evenings, on the
   lineless, level floors;
Through the yelling Channel tempest when the
   siren hoots and roars –
By day the dipping house-flag and by night the
   rocket's trail –
As the sheep that graze behind us so we know
   them where they hail.

We bridge across the dark, and bid the helmsman
   have a care,
The flash that, wheeling inland, wakes his sleeping
   wife to prayer.
From our vexed eyries, head to gale, we bind in
   burning chains

The lover from the sea-rim drawn – his love in
     English lanes.

We greet the clippers wing-and-wing that race the
     Southern wool;
We warn the crawling cargo-tanks of Bremen,
     Leith, and Hull;
To each and all our equal lamp at peril of the sea –
The white wall-sided warships or the whalers of
     Dundee!

Come up, come in from Eastward, from the
     guardports of the Morn!
Beat up, beat in from Southerly, O gypsies of the
     Horn!
Swift shuttles of an Empire's loom that weave us
     main to main,
The Coastwise Lights of England give you
     welcome back again!

Go, get you gone up-Channel with the sea-crust
     on your plates;
Go, get you into London with the burden of your
     freights!
Haste, for they talk of Empire there, and say, if
     any seek,
The Lights of England sent you and by silence
     shall ye speak!

THE SONG OF THE DEAD

*Hear now the Song of the Dead – in the North by the
    torn berg-edges –*
*They that look still to the Pole, asleep by their hide-
    stripped sledges.*
*Song of the Dead in the South – in the sun by their
    skeleton horses,*
*Where the warrigal whimpers and bays through the
    dust of the sere river-courses.*

*Song of the Dead in the East – in the heat-rotted
    jungle-hollows,*
*Where the dog-ape barks in the kloof – in the brake of
    the buffalo-wallows.*
*Song of the Dead in the West – in the Barrens, the
    pass that betrayed them;*
*Where the wolverine tumbles their packs from the
    camp and the grave-mound they made them;*
        Hear now the Song of the Dead!

I

We were dreamers, dreaming greatly, in the man-
    stifled town;
We yearned beyond the skyline where the strange
    roads go down.
Came the Whisper, came the Vision, came the
    Power with the Need,
Till the Soul that is not man's soul was lent us to
    lead.

As the deer breaks – as the steer breaks – from
    the herd where they graze,
In the faith of little children we went on our ways.
Then the wood failed – then the food failed –
    then the last water dried –

In the faith of little children we lay down and died.
On the sand-drift – on the veldt-side – in the fern-
scrub we lay,
That our sons might follow after by the bones on
the way.
Follow after – follow after! We have watered the
root,
And the bud has come to blossom that ripens for
fruit!
Follow after – we are waiting, by the trails that we
lost,
For the sounds of many footsteps, for the tread of
a host.
Follow after – follow after – for the harvest is sown:
By the bones about the wayside ye shall come to
your own!

When Drake went down to the Horn
And England was crowned thereby,
'Twixt seas unsailed and shores unhailed
Our Lodge – our Lodge was born
(And England was crowned thereby!)

Which never shall close again
By day nor yet by night,
While man shall take his life to stake
At risk of shoal or main
(By day nor yet by night)

But standeth even so
As now we witness here,
While men depart, of joyful heart,
Adventure for to know
(As now bear witness here!)

We have fed our sea for a thousand years
    And she calls us, still unfed,
Though there's never a wave of all her waves
    But marks our English dead:
We have strawed our best to the weed's unrest,
    To the shark and the sheering gull.
If blood be the price of admiralty,
    Lord God, we ha' paid in full!

There's never a flood goes shoreward now
    But lifts a keel we manned;
There's never an ebb goes seaward now
    But drops our dead on the sand –
But slinks our dead on the sands forlore,
    From the Ducies to the Swin.
If blood be the price of admiralty,
If blood be the price of admiralty,
    Lord God, we ha' paid it in!

We must feed our sea for a thousand years,
    For that is our doom and pride,
As it was when they sailed with the *Golden Hind*,
    Or the wreck that struck last tide –
Or the wreck that lies on the spouting reef
    Where the ghastly blue-lights flare.
If blood be the price of admiralty,
If blood be the price of admiralty,
If blood be the price of admiralty,
    Lord God, we ha' bought it fair!

THE DEEP-SEA CABLES

The wrecks dissolve above us; their dust drops
    down from afar –
Down to the dark, to the utter dark, where the
    blind white sea-snakes are.
There is no sound, no echo of sound, in the
    deserts of the deep,
Or the great grey level plains of ooze where the
    shell-burred cables creep.

Here in the womb of the world – here on the tie-
    ribs of earth
Words, and the words of men, flicker and flutter
    and beat –
Warning, sorrow, and gain, salutation and mirth –
For a Power troubles the Still that has neither
    voice nor feet.

They have wakened the timeless Things; they
    have killed their father Time;
Joining hands in the gloom, a league from the last
    of the sun.
Hush! Men talk today o'er the waste of the
    ultimate slime,
And a new Word runs between: whispering, 'Let
    us be one!'

THE SONG OF THE SONS

One from the ends of the earth – gifts at an open
    door –
Treason has much, but we, Mother, thy sons have
    more!
From the whine of a dying man, from the snarl of
    a wolf-pack freed,
Turn, and the world is thine. Mother, be proud of
    thy seed!
Count, are we feeble or few? Hear, is our speech
    so rude?
Look, are we poor in the land? Judge, are we men
    of The Blood?

Those that have stayed at thy knees, Mother, go
    call them in –
We that were bred overseas wait and would speak
    with our kin.
Not in the dark do we fight – haggle and flout and
    gibe;
Selling our love for a price, loaning our hearts for
    a bribe.
Gifts have we only today – Love without promise
    or fee –
Hear, for thy children speak, from the uttermost
    parts of the sea!

THE SONG OF THE CITIES

BOMBAY

Royal and Dower-royal, I the Queen
    Fronting thy richest sea with richer hands –
A thousand mills roar through me where I glean
    All races from all lands.

CALCUTTA

Me the Sea-captain loved, the River built,
    Wealth sought and Kings adventured life to
      hold.
Hail, England! I am Asia – Power on silt,
    Death in my hands, but Gold!

MADRAS

Clive kissed me on the mouth and eyes and brow,
    Wonderful kisses, so that I became
Crowned above Queens – a withered beldame now
    Brooding on ancient fame.

RANGOON

Hail, Mother! Do they call me rich in trade?
    Little care I, but hear the shorn priest drone,
And watch my silk-clad lovers, man by maid,
    Laugh 'neath my Shwe Dagon.

SINGAPORE

Hail, Mother! East and West must seek my aid
    Ere the spent hull may dare the ports afar.
The second doorway of the wide world's trade
    Is mine to loose or bar.

HONG-KONG

Hail, Mother! Hold me fast; my Praya sleeps
   Under innumerable keels today.
Yet guard (and landward), or tomorrow sweeps
   Thy warships down the bay!

HALIFAX

Into the mist my guardian prows put forth,
   Behind the mist my virgin ramparts lie,
The Warden of the Honour of the North,
   Sleepless and veiled am I!

QUEBEC AND MONTREAL

Peace is our portion. Yet a whisper rose,
   Foolish and causeless, half in jest, half hate.
Now wake we and remember mighty blows,
   And, fearing no man, wait!

VICTORIA

From East to West the circling word has passed,
   Till West is East beside our landlocked blue;
From East to West the tested chain holds fast,
   The well-forged link rings true!

CAPE TOWN

Hail! Snatched and bartered oft from hand to hand,
   I dream my dream, by rock and heath and pine,
Of Empire to the northward. Ay, one land
   From Lion's Head to Line!

MELBOURNE

Greeting! Nor fear nor favour won us place,
  Got between greed of gold and dread of drouth,
Loud-voiced and reckless as the wild tide-race
  That whips our harbour-mouth!

SYDNEY

Greeting! My birth-stain have I turned to good;
  Forcing strong wills perverse to steadfastness:
The first flush of the tropics in my blood,
  And at my feet Success!

BRISBANE

The northern stock beneath the southern skies –
  I build a Nation for an Empire's need,
Suffer a little, and my land shall rise,
  Queen over lands indeed!

HOBART

Man's love first found me; man's hate made me Hell;
  For my babes' sake I cleansed those infamies.
Earnest for leave to live and labour well,
  God flung me peace and ease.

AUCKLAND

Last, loneliest, loveliest, exquisite, apart –
  On us, on us the unswerving season smiles,
Who wonder 'mid our fern why men depart
  To seek the Happy Isles!

Truly ye come of The Blood; slower to bless than
    to ban,
Little used to lie down at the bidding of any man –
Flesh of the flesh that I bred, bone of the bone
    that I bare;
Stark as your sons shall be – stern as your fathers
    were.
Deeper than speech our love, stronger than life
    our tether,
But we do not fall on the neck nor kiss when we
    come together.
My arm is nothing weak, my strength is not gone by;
Sons, I have borne many sons, but my dugs are
    not dry.
Look, I have made ye a place and opened wide
    the doors,
That ye may talk together, your Barons and
    Councillors –
Wards of the Outer March, Lords of the Lower
    Seas,
Ay, talk to your grey mother that bore you on her
    knees! –
That ye may talk together, brother to brother's
    face –
Thus for the good of your peoples – thus for the
    Pride of the Race.
Also, we will make promise. So long as The Blood
    endures,
I shall know that your good is mine: ye shall feel
    that my strength is yours:
In the day of Armageddon, at the last great fight
    of all,

That Our House stand together and the pillars do
not fall.
Draw now the threefold knot firm on the ninefold
bands,
And the Law that ye make shall be law after the
rule of your lands.
This for the waxen Heath, and that for the
Wattle-bloom,
This for the Maple-leaf, and that for the Southern
Broom.
The Law that ye make shall be law and I do not
press my will,
Because ye are Sons of The Blood and call me
Mother still.
Now must ye speak to your kinsmen and they
must speak to you,
After the use of the English, in straight-flung
words and few.
Go to your work and be strong, halting not in
your ways,
Baulking the end half-won for an instant dole of
praise.
Stand to your work and be wise – certain of sword
and pen,
Who are neither children nor Gods, but men in a
world of men!

1893

The Gypsy Trail

The white moth to the closing bine,
  The bee to the opened clover,
And the gypsy blood to the gypsy blood
  Ever the wide world over.

Ever the wide world over, lass,
  Ever the trail held true,
Over the world and under the world,
  And back at the last to you.

Out of the dark of the gorgio camp,
  Out of the grime and the grey
(Morning waits at the end of the world),
  Gypsy, come away!

The wild boar to the sun-dried swamp,
  The red crane to her reed,
And the Romany lass to the Romany lad
  By the tie of a roving breed.

The pied snake to the rifted rock,
  The buck to the stony plain,
And the Romany lass to the Romany lad,
  And both to the road again.

Both to the road again, again!
  Out on a clean sea-track –
Follow the cross of the gypsy trail
  Over the world and back!

Follow the Romany patteran
  North where the blue bergs sail,
And the bows are grey with the frozen spray,
  And the masts are shod with mail.

Follow the Romany patteran
  Sheer to the Austral Light,
Where the besom of God is the wild South wind,
  Sweeping the sea-floors white.

Follow the Romany patteran
  West to the sinking sun,
Till the junk-sails lift through the houseless drift,
  And the east and the west are one.

Follow the Romany patteran
  East where the silence broods
By a purple wave on an opal beach
  In the hush of the Mahim woods.

'The wild hawk to the windswept sky,
  The deer to the wholesome wold,
And the heart of a man to the heart of a maid,
  As it was in the days of old.'

The heart of a man to the heart of a maid –
  Light of my tents, be fleet.
Morning waits at the end of the world,
  And the world is all at our feet!

The Irish Guards

We're not so old in the Army List,
   But we're not so young at our trade,
For we had the honour at Fontenoy
   Of meeting the Guards' Brigade.
'Twas Lally, Dillon, Bulkeley, Clare,
   And Lee that led us then,
And after a hundred and seventy years
   We're fighting for France again!
     Old Days! The wild geese are flighting,
       Head to the storm as they faced it before!
     For where there are Irish there's bound to be
       fighting,
       And when there's no fighting, it's Ireland
       no more!
              Ireland no more!

The fashion's all for khaki now,
   But once through France we went
Full-dressed in scarlet Army cloth
   The English – left at Ghent.
They're fighting on our side today
   But, before they changed their clothes,
The half of Europe knew our fame,
   As all of Ireland knows!
     Old Days! The wild geese are flying,
       Head to the storm as they faced it before!
     For where there are Irish there's memory
       undying,
       And when we forget, it is Ireland no more!
       Ireland no more!

From Barry Wood to Gouzeaucourt,
    From Boyne to Pilkem Ridge,
The ancient days come back no more
    Than water under the bridge.
But the bridge it stands and the water runs
    As red as yesterday,
And the Irish move to the sound of the guns
    Like salmon to the sea.
        Old Days! The wild geese are ranging,
            Head to the storm as they faced it before!
        For where there are Irish their hearts are
            unchanging,
        And when they are changed, it is Ireland no more!
                    Ireland no more!

We're not so old in the Army List,
    But we're not so new in the ring,
For we carried our packs with Marshal Saxe
    When Louis was our King.
But Douglas Haig's our Marshal now
    And we're King George's men,
And after one hundred and seventy years
    We're fighting for France again!
        Ah, France! And did we stand by you,
            When life was made splendid with gifts
                and rewards?
        Ah, France! And will we deny you
            In the hour of your agony, Mother of Swords?
        Old Days! The wild geese are flighting,
            Head to the storm as they faced it before!
        For where there are Irish there's loving and
            fighting,
        And when we stop either, it's Ireland no more!
                    Ireland no more!

                                        1918

The Settler

Here, where my fresh-turned furrows run,
  And the deep soil glistens red,
I will repair the wrong that was done
  To the living and the dead.
Here, where the senseless bullet fell,
  And the barren shrapnel burst,
I will plant a tree, I will dig a well,
  Against the heat and the thirst.

Here, in a large and a sunlit land,
  Where no wrong bites to the bone,
I will lay my hand in my neighbour's hand,
  And together we will atone
For the set folly and the red breach
  And the black waste of it all;
Giving and taking counsel each
  Over the cattle-kraal.

Here will we join against our foes —
  The hailstroke and the storm,
And the red and rustling cloud that blows
  The locust's mile-deep swarm.
Frost and murrain and flood let loose
  Shall launch us side by side
In the holy wars that have no truce
  'Twixt seed and harvest-tide.

Earth, where we rode to slay or be slain,
  Our love shall redeem unto life.
We will gather and lead to her lips again
  The waters of ancient strife,

From the far and the fiercely guarded streams
    And the pools where we lay in wait,
Till the corn cover our evil dreams
    And the young corn our hate.

And when we bring old fights to mind,
    We will not remember the sin –
If there be blood on his head of my kind,
    Or blood on my head of his kin –
For the ungrazed upland, the untilled lea
    Cry, and the fields forlorn:
'The dead must bury their dead, but ye –
    Ye serve an host unborn.'

Bless then, Our God, the new-yoked plough
    And the good beasts that draw,
And the bread we eat in the sweat of our brow
    According to Thy Law.
After us cometh a multitude –
    Prosper the work of our hands,
That we may feed with our Land's food
    The folk of all our lands!

Here, in the waves and the troughs of the plains,
    Where the healing stillness lies,
And the vast, benignant sky restrains
    And the long days make wise –
Bless to our use the rain and the sun
    And the blind seed in its bed,
That we may repair the wrong that was done
    To the living and the dead!

1903
South African War ended, May 1902

Sussex

God gave all men all earth to love,
    But, since our hearts are small,
Ordained for each one spot should prove
    Belovèd over all;
That, as He watched Creation's birth,
    So we, in godlike mood,
May of our love create our earth
    And see that it is good.

So one shall Baltic pines content,
    As one some Surrey glade,
Or one the palm-grove's droned lament
    Before Levuka's Trade.
Each to his choice, and I rejoice
    The lot has fallen to me
In a fair ground – in a fair ground –
    Yea, Sussex by the sea!

No tenderhearted garden crowns,
    No bosomed woods adorn
Our blunt, bow-headed, whale-backed Downs,
    But gnarled and writhen thorn –
Bare slopes where chasing shadows skim,
    And, through the gaps revealed,
Belt upon belt, the wooded, dim,
    Blue goodness of the Weald.

Clean of officious fence or hedge,
    Half-wild and wholly tame,
The wise turf cloaks the white cliff-edge
    As when the Romans came.

What sign of those that fought and died
　　At shift of sword and sword?
The barrow and the camp abide,
　　The sunlight and the sward.

Here leaps ashore the full Sou'west
　　All heavy-winged with brine,
Here lies above the folded crest
　　The Channel's leaden line;
And here the sea-fogs lap and cling,
　　And here, each warning each,
The sheep-bells and the ship-bells ring
　　Along the hidden beach.

We have no waters to delight
　　Our broad and brookless vales –
Only the dewpond on the height
　　Unfed, that never fails –
Whereby no tattered herbage tells
　　Which way the season flies –
Only our close-bit thyme that smells
　　Like dawn in Paradise.

Here through the strong and shadeless days
　　The tinkling silence thrills;
Or little, lost, Down churches praise
　　The Lord who made the hills:
But here the Old Gods guard their round,
　　And, in her secret heart,
The heathen kingdom Wilfrid found
　　Dreams, as she dwells, apart.

Though all the rest were all my share,
　　With equal soul I'd see

Her nine-and-thirty sisters fair,
    Yet none more fair than she.
Choose ye your need from Thames to Tweed,
    And I will choose instead
Such lands as lie 'twixt Rake and Rye,
    Black Down and Beachy Head.

I will go out against the sun
    Where the rolled scarp retires,
And the Long Man of Wilmington
    Looks naked toward the shires;
And east till doubling Rother crawls
    To find the fickle tide,
By dry and sea-forgotten walls,
    Our ports of stranded pride.

I will go north about the shaws
    And the deep ghylls that breed
Huge oaks and old, the which we hold
    No more than Sussex weed;
Or south where windy Piddinghoe's
    Begilded dolphin veers,
And red beside wide-banked Ouse
    Lie down our Sussex steers.

So to the land our hearts we give
    Till the sure magic strike,
And Memory, Use, and Love make live
    Us and our fields alike –
That deeper than our speech and thought,
    Beyond our reason's sway,
Clay of the pit whence we were wrought
    Yearns to its fellow-clay.

God gives all men all earth to love,
  But, since man's heart is small,
Ordains for each one spot shall prove
  Beloved over all.
Each to his choice, and I rejoice
  The lot has fallen to me
In a fair ground – in a fair ground –
  Yea, Sussex by the sea!

1902

My Boy Jack

'Have you news of my boy Jack?'
  Not this tide.
'When d'you think that he'll come back?'
  Not with this wind blowing, and this tide.

'Has anyone else had word of him?'
  Not this tide.
For what is sunk will hardly swim,
  Not with this wind blowing, and this tide.

'Oh, dear, what comfort can I find?'
  None this tide,
  Nor any tide,
Except he did not shame his kind –
  Not even with that wind blowing, and that tide.

Then hold your head up all the more,
  This tide,
  And every tide;
Because he was the son you bore,
  And gave to that wind blowing and that tide!

                                    1914–18

The Vampire

A fool there was and he made his prayer
(Even as you and I!)
To a rag and a bone and a hank of hair
(We called her the woman who did not care)
But the fool he called her his lady fair –
(Even as you and I!)

Oh, the years we waste and the tears we waste
And the work of our head and hand
Belong to the woman who did not know
(And now we know that she never could know)
And did not understand!

A fool there was and his goods he spent
(Even as you and I!)
Honour and faith and a sure intent
(And it wasn't the least what the lady meant)
But a fool must follow his natural bent
(Even as you and I!)

Oh, the toil we lost and the spoil we lost
And the excellent things we planned
Belong to the woman who didn't know why
(And now we know that she never knew why)
And did not understand!

The fool was stripped to his foolish hide
(Even as you and I!)
Which she might have seen when she threw him
    aside –
(But it isn't on record the lady tried)
So some of him lived but the most of him died –
(Even as you and I!)

And it isn't the shame and it isn't the blame
That stings like a white-hot brand –
It's coming to know that she never knew why
(Seeing, at last, she could never know why)
And never could understand!

1897

When Earth's Last Picture is Painted

When Earth's last picture is painted and the tubes
  are twisted and dried,
When the oldest colours have faded, and the
  youngest critic has died,
We shall rest, and, faith, we shall need it – lie
  down for an æon or two,
Till the Master of All Good Workmen shall put us
  to work anew.

And those that were good shall be happy: they
  shall sit in a golden chair;
They shall splash at a ten-league canvas with
  brushes of comets' hair.
They shall find real saints to draw from – Magdalene,
  Peter, and Paul;
They shall work for an age at a sitting and never
  be tired at all!

And only The Master shall praise us, and only
  The Master shall blame;
And no one shall work for money, and no one
  shall work for fame,
But each for the joy of the working, and each, in
  his separate star,
Shall draw the Thing as he sees It for the God of
  Things as They are!

1892
L'Envoi to 'The Seven Seas'

The Ballad of East and West

*Oh, East is East, and West is West, and never the
    twain shall meet,*
*Till Earth and Sky stand presently at God's great
    Judgment Seat;*
*But there is neither East nor West, Border, nor Breed,
    nor Birth,*
*When two strong men stand face to face, though they
    come from the ends of the earth!*

Kamal is out with twenty men to raise the Border-
    side,
And he has lifted the Colonel's mare that is the
    Colonel's pride.
He has lifted her out of the stable-door between
    the dawn and the day,
And turned the calkins upon her feet, and ridden
    her far away.
Then up and spoke the Colonel's son that led a
    troop of the Guides:
'Is there never a man of all my men can say where
    Kamal hides?'
Then up and spoke Mohammed Khan, the son of
    the Ressaldar:
'If ye know the track of the morning-mist, ye
    know where his pickets are.
At dusk he harries the Abazai – at dawn he is into
    Bonair,
But he must go by Fort Bukloh to his own place
    to fare.
So if ye gallop to Fort Bukloh as fast as a bird can
    fly,

By the favour of God ye may cut him off ere he
    win to the Tongue of Jagai.
But if he be past the Tongue of Jagai, right swiftly
    turn ye then,
For the length and the breadth of that grisly plain
    is sown with Kamal's men.
There is rock to the left, and rock to the right, and
    low lean thorn between,
And ye may hear a breech-bolt snick where never
    a man is seen.'
The Colonel's son has taken horse, and a raw
    rough dun was he,
With the mouth of a bell and the heart of Hell and
    the head of a gallows-tree.
The Colonel's son to the Fort has won, they bid
    him stay to eat –
Who rides at the tail of a Border thief, he sits not
    long at his meat.
He's up and away from Fort Bukloh as fast as he
    can fly,
Till he was aware of his father's mare in the gut of
    the Tongue of Jagai,
Till he was aware of his father's mare with Kamal
    upon her back,
And when he could spy the white of her eye, he
    made the pistol crack.
He has fired once, he has fired twice, but the
    whistling ball went wide.
'Ye shoot like a soldier,' Kamal said. 'Show now if
    ye can ride!'
It's up and over the Tongue of Jagai, as blown
    dust-devils go.
The dun he fled like a stag of ten, but the mare
    like a barren doe.

The dun he leaned against the bit and slugged his
    head above,
But the red mare played with the snaffle-bars, as a
    maiden plays with a glove.
There was rock to the left and rock to the right,
    and low lean thorn between,
And thrice he heard a breech-bolt snick tho' never
    a man was seen.
They have ridden the low moon out of the sky,
    their hoofs drum up the dawn,
The dun he went like a wounded bull, but the
    mare like a new-roused fawn.
The dun he fell at a watercourse – in a woeful
    heap fell he,
And Kamal has turned the red mare back, and
    pulled the rider free.
He has knocked the pistol out of his hand – small
    room was there to strive,
' 'Twas only by favour of mine,' quoth he, 'ye
    rode so long alive:
There was not a rock for twenty mile, there was
    not a clump of tree,
But covered a man of my own men with his rifle
    cocked on his knee.
If I had raised my bridle-hand, as I have held it
    low,
The little jackals that flee so fast were feasting all
    in a row.
If I had bowed my head on my breast, as I have
    held it high,
The kite that whistles above us now were gorged
    till she could not fly.'
Lightly answered the Colonel's son: 'Do good to
    bird and beast,

But count who come for the broken meats before
    thou makest a feast.
If there should follow a thousand swords to carry
    my bones away,
Belike the price of a jackal's meal were more than
    a thief could pay.
They will feed their horse on the standing crop,
    their men on the garnered grain.
The thatch of the byres will serve their fires when
    all the cattle are slain.
But if thou thinkest the price be fair, – thy
    brethren wait to sup,
The hound is kin to the jackal-spawn, – howl,
    dog, and call them up!
And if thou thinkest the price be high, in steer and
    gear and stack,
Give me my father's mare again, and I'll fight my
    own way back!'
Kamal has gripped him by the hand and set him
    upon his feet.
'No talk shall be of dogs,' said he, 'when wolf and
    grey wolf meet.
May I eat dirt if thou hast hurt of me in deed or
    breath;
What dam of lances brought thee forth to jest at
    the dawn with Death?'
Lightly answered the Colonel's son: 'I hold by the
    blood of my clan:
Take up the mare for my father's gift – by God,
    she has carried a man!'
The red mare ran to the Colonel's son, and
    nuzzled against his breast;
'We be two strong men,' said Kamal then, 'but
    she loveth the younger best.

So she shall go with a lifter's dower, my turquoise-
    studded rein,
My 'broidered saddle and saddle-cloth, and silver
    stirrups twain.'
The Colonel's son a pistol drew, and held it
    muzzle-end,
'Ye have taken the one from a foe,' said he. 'Will
    ye take the mate from a friend?'
'A gift for a gift,' said Kamal straight; 'a limb for
    the risk of a limb.
'Thy father has sent his son to me, I'll send my
    son to him!'
With that he whistled his only son, that dropped
    from a mountain-crest –
He trod the ling like a buck in spring, and he
    looked like a lance in rest.
'Now here is thy master,' Kamal said, 'who leads
    a troop of the Guides,
And thou must ride at his left side as shield on
    shoulder rides.
Till Death or I cut loose the tie, at camp and
    board and bed,
Thy life is his – thy fate it is to guard him with thy
    head.
So, thou must eat the White Queen's meat, and
    all her foes are thine,
And thou must harry thy father's hold for the
    peace of the Borderline.
And thou must make a trooper tough and hack
    thy way to power –
Belike they will raise thee to Ressaldar when I am
    hanged in Peshawur!'

They have looked each other between the eyes,
    and there they found no fault.
They have taken the Oath of the Brother-in-Blood
    on leavened bread and salt:
They have taken the Oath of the Brother-in-Blood
    on fire and fresh-cut sod,
On the hilt and the haft of the Khyber knife, and
    the Wondrous Names of God.
The Colonel's son he rides the mare and Kamal's
    boy the dun,
And two have come back to Fort Bukloh where
    there went forth but one.
And when they drew to the Quarter-Guard, full
    twenty swords flew clear –
There was not a man but carried his feud with the
    blood of the mountaineer.
'Ha' done! ha' done!' said the Colonel's son. 'Put
    up the steel at your sides!
Last night ye had struck at a Border thief –
    tonight 'tis a man of the Guides!'

Oh, East is East, and West is West, and never the
    twain shall meet,
Till Earth and Sky stand presently at God's great
    Judgment Seat;
But there is neither East nor West, Border, nor Breed,
    nor Birth,
When two strong men stand face to face, though they
    come from the ends of the earth!

1889

Gehazi

Whence comest thou, Gehazi,
   So reverend to behold,
In scarlet and in ermines
   And chain of England's gold?
'From following after Naaman
   To tell him all is well,
Whereby my zeal hath made me
   A Judge in Israel.'

Well done, well done, Gehazi!
   Stretch forth thy ready hand.
Thou barely 'scaped from judgment,
   Take oath to judge the land
Unswayed by gift of money
   Or privy bribe, more base;
Of knowledge which is profit
   In any marketplace.

Search out and probe, Gehazi,
   As thou of all canst try,
The truthful, well-weighed answer
   That tells the blacker lie –
The loud, uneasy virtue,
   The anger feigned at will,
To overbear a witness
   And make the Court keep still.

Take order now, Gehazi,
   That no man talk aside
In secret with his judges
   The while his case is tried.

Lest he should show them – reason
　　To keep a matter hid,
And subtly lead the questions
　　Away from what he did.

Thou mirror of uprightness,
　　What ails thee at thy vows?
What means the risen whiteness
　　Of the skin between thy brows?
The boils that shine and burrow,
　　The sores that slough and bleed –
The leprosy of Naaman
　　On thee and all thy seed?
　　　Stand up, stand up, Gehazi,
　　　　Draw close thy robe and go,
　　Gehazi, Judge in Israel,
　　　A leper white as snow!

1915

Et Dona Ferentes

In extended observation of the ways and works of
    man,
From the Four-mile Radius roughly to the Plains
    of Hindustan:
I have drunk with mixed assemblies, seen the
    racial ruction rise,
And the men of half Creation damning half
    Creation's eyes.

I have watched them in their tantrums, all that
    pentecostal crew,
French, Italian, Arab, Spaniard, Dutch and
    Greek, and Russ and Jew,
Celt and savage, buff and ochre, cream and
    yellow, mauve and white,
But it never really mattered till the English grew
    polite;

Till the men with polished toppers, till the men in
    long frock-coats,
Till the men who do not duel, till the men who
    war with votes,
Till the breed that take their pleasures as Saint
    Lawrence took his grid,
Began to 'beg your pardon' and – the knowing
    croupier hid.

Then the bandsmen with their fiddles, and the
    girls that bring the beer,
Felt the psychological moment, left the lit Casino
    clear;
But the uninstructed alien, from the Teuton to
    the Gaul,

Was entrapped, once more, my country, by that
    suave, deceptive drawl.

*   *   *

As it was in ancient Suez or 'neath wilder, milder
    skies,
I 'observe with apprehension' how the racial
    ructions rise;
And with keener apprehension, if I read the times
    aright,
Hear the old Casino order: 'Watch your man, but
    be polite.

'Keep your temper. Never answer (*that* was why
    they spat and swore).
Don't hit first, but move together (there's no
    hurry) to the door.
Back to back, and facing outward while the
    linguist tells 'em how –
"*Nous sommes allong ar notre batteau, nous ne
    voulong pas un row.*" '

So the hard, pent rage ate inward, till some idiot
    went too far . . .
'Let 'em have it!' and they had it, and the same
    was merry war –
Fist, umbrella, cane, decanter, lamp and beer-
    mug, chair and boot –
Till behind the fleeing legions rose the long,
    hoarse yell for loot.

Then the oilcloth with its numbers, like a banner
    fluttered free;
Then the grand piano cantered, on three castors,
    down the quay;

White, and breathing through their nostrils, silent,
    systematic, swift –
They removed, effaced, abolished all that man
    could heave or lift.

Oh, my country, bless the training that from cot
    to castle runs –
The pitfall of the stranger but the bulwark of thy
    sons –
Measured speech and ordered action, sluggish
    soul and unperturbed,
Till we wake our Island-Devil – nowise cool for
    being curbed!

When the heir of all the ages 'has the honour to
    remain,'
When he will not hear an insult, though men
    make it ne'er so plain,
When his lips are schooled to meekness, when his
    back is bowed to blows –
Well the keen *aas-vogels* know it – well the waiting
    jackal knows.

Build on the flanks of Etna where the sullen
    smoke-puffs float –
Or bathe in tropic waters where the lean fin dogs
    the boat –
Cock the gun that is not loaded, cook the frozen
    dynamite –
But oh, beware my Country, when my Country
    grows polite!

1896

The Holy War

'For here lay the excellent wisdom of him that built Mansoul, that the walls could never be broken down nor hurt by the most mighty adverse potentate unless the townsmen gave consent thereto.'

Bunyan's *Holy War*

A tinker out of Bedford,
    A vagrant oft in quod,
A private under Fairfax,
    A minister of God –
Two hundred years and thirty
    Ere Armageddon came
His single hand portrayed it,
    And Bunyan was his name!

He mapped for those who follow,
    The world in which we are –
'This famous town of Mansoul'
    That takes the Holy War.
Her true and traitor people,
    The Gates along her wall,
From Eye Gate unto Feel Gate,
    John Bunyan showed them all.

All enemy divisions,
    Recruits of every class,
And highly screened positions
    For flame or poison-gas;
The craft that we call modern,
    The crimes that we call new,
John Bunyan had 'em typed and filed
    In Sixteen Eighty-two.

Likewise the Lords of Looseness
   That hamper faith and works,
The Perseverance-Doubters,
   And Present-Comfort shirks,
With brittle intellectuals
   Who crack beneath a strain –
John Bunyan met that helpful set
   In Charles the Second's reign.

Emmanuel's vanguard dying
   For right and not for rights,
My Lord Apollyon lying
   To the State-kept Stockholmites,
The Pope, the swithering Neutrals,
   The Kaiser and his Gott –
Their rôles, their goals, their naked souls –
   He knew and drew the lot.

Now he hath left his quarters,
   In Bunhill Fields to lie,
The wisdom that he taught us
   Is proven prophecy –
One watchword through our Armies,
   One answer from our Lands: –
'No dealings with Diabolus
   As long as Mansoul stands!'

A pedlar from a hovel,
   The lowest of the low –
The Father of the Novel,
   Salvation's first Defoe –
Eight blinded generations
   Ere Armageddon came,
He showed us how to meet it,
   And Bunyan was his name!

1917

France

Broke to every known mischance, lifted over all
By the light sane joy of life, the buckler of the Gaul;
Furious in luxury, merciless in toil,
Terrible with strength that draws from her tireless soil;
Strictest judge of her own worth, gentlest of man's
    mind,
First to follow Truth and last to leave old Truths
    behind –
France, beloved of every soul that loves its fellow-kind!

Ere our birth (rememberest thou?) side by side we
    lay
Fretting in the womb of Rome to begin our fray.
Ere men knew our tongues apart, our one task
    was known –
Each to mould the other's fate as he wrought his
    own.
To this end we stirred mankind till all Earth was
    ours,
Till our world-end strifes begat wayside Thrones
    and Powers –
Puppets that we made or broke to bar the other's
    path –
Necessary, outpost-folk, hirelings of our wrath.
To this end we stormed the seas, tack for tack,
    and burst
Through the doorways of new worlds, doubtful
    which was first,
Hand on hilt (rememberest thou?) ready for the
    blow –
Sure, whatever else we met, we should meet our foe.

Spurred or balked at every stride by the other's
  strength,
So we rode the ages down and every ocean's
  length!

Where did you refrain from us or we refrain from
  you?
Ask the wave that has not watched war between
  us two!
Others held us for a while, but with weaker
  charms,
These we quitted at the call for each other's arms.

Eager toward the known delight, equally we
  strove –
Each the other's mystery, terror, need, and love.
To each other's open court with our proofs we
  came.
Where could we find honour else, or men to test
  our claim?
From each other's throat we wrenched – valour's
  last reward –
That extorted word of praise gasped 'twixt lunge
  and guard.
In each other's cup we poured mingled blood and
  tears,
Brutal joys, unmeasured hopes, intolerable fears –
All that soiled or salted life for a thousand years.
Proved beyond the need of proof, matched in
  every clime,
O Companion, we have lived greatly through all
  time!

Yoked in knowledge and remorse, now we come
to rest,
Laughing at old villainies that Time has turned to
jest;
Pardoning old necessities no pardon can efface –
That undying sin we shared in Rouen
marketplace.

Now we watch the new years shape, wondering if
they hold
Fiercer lightnings in their heart than we launched
of old.
Now we hear new voices rise, question, boast or
gird,
As we raged (rememberest thou?) when our
crowds were stirred.
Now we count new keels afloat, and new hosts on
land,
Massed like ours (rememberest thou?) when our
strokes were planned.
We were schooled for dear life's sake, to know
each other's blade.
What can Blood and Iron make more than we
have made?
We have learned by keenest use to know each
other's mind.
What shall Blood and Iron loose that we cannot
bind?
We who swept each other's coast, sacked each
other's home,
Since the sword of Brennus clashed on the scales
at Rome,
Listen, count and close again, wheeling girth to
girth,

In the linked and steadfast guard set for peace on
      earth!

Broke to every known mischance, lifted over all
By the light sane joy of life, the buckler of the
      Gaul;
Furious in luxury, merciless in toil,
Terrible with strength renewed from a tireless soil;
Strictest judge of her own worth, gentlest of man's
      mind,
First to face the Truth and last to leave old Truths
      behind –
France, beloved of every soul that loves or serves
      its kind!

Mesopotamia

They shall not return to us, the resolute, the young,
    The eager and wholehearted whom we gave:
But the men who left them thriftily to die in their
    own dung,
      Shall they come with years and honour to the
      grave?

They shall not return to us, the strong men coldly
    slain
    In sight of help denied from day to day:
But the men who edged their agonies and chid
    them in their pain,
      Are they too strong and wise to put away?

Our dead shall not return to us while Day and
    Night divide –
    Never while the bars of sunset hold.
But the idle-minded overlings who quibbled while
    they died,
      Shall they thrust for high employments as of old?

Shall we only threaten and be angry for an hour?
    When the storm is ended shall we find
How softly but how swiftly they have sidled back
    to power
      By the favour and contrivance of their kind?

Even while they soothe us, while they promise
    large amends,
    Even while they make a show of fear,
Do they call upon their debtors, and take counsel
    with their friends,
      To confirm and re-establish each career?

Their lives cannot repay us – their death could not
   undo –
   The shame that they have laid upon our race.
But the slothfulness that wasted and the arrogance
   that slew,
   Shall we leave it unabated in its place?

1917

The Islanders

No Doubt but ye are the People – your throne is above the King's.
Whoso speaks in your presence must say acceptable things:
Bowing the head in worship, bending the knee in fear –
Bringing the word well smoothen – such as a King should hear.

Fenced by your careful fathers, ringed by your leaden seas,
Long did ye wake in quiet and long lie down at ease;
Till ye said of Strife, 'What is it?' of the Sword, 'It is far from our ken';
Till ye made a sport of your shrunken hosts and a toy of your armèd men.
Ye stopped your ears to the warning – ye would neither look nor heed –
Ye set your leisure before their toil and your lusts above their need.
Because of your witless learning and your beasts of warren and chase,
Ye grudged your sons to their service and your fields for their camping-place.
Ye forced them glean in the highways the straw for the bricks they brought;
Ye forced them follow in byways the craft that ye never taught.
Ye hampered and hindered and crippled; ye thrust out of sight and away
Those that would serve you for honour and those that served you for pay.

Then were the judgments loosened; then was your
    shame revealed,
At the hands of a little people, few but apt in the
    field.
Yet ye were saved by a remnant (and your land's
    long-suffering star),
When your strong men cheered in their millions
    while your striplings went to the war.
Sons of the sheltered city – unmade, unhandled,
    unmeet –
Ye pushed them raw to the battle as ye picked
    them raw from the street.
And what did ye look they should compass?
    Warcraft learned in a breath,
Knowledge unto occasion at the first far view of
    Death?
So? And ye train your horses and the dogs ye feed
    and prize?
How are the beasts more worthy than the souls,
    your sacrifice?
But ye said, 'Their valour shall show them'; but ye
    said, 'The end is close.'
And ye sent them comfits and pictures to help
    them harry your foes:
And ye vaunted your fathomless power, and ye
    flaunted your iron pride,
Ere – ye fawned on the Younger Nations for the
    men who could shoot and ride!
Then ye returned to your trinkets; then ye contented
    your souls
With the flannelled fools at the wicket or the
    muddied oafs at the goals.
Given to strong delusion, wholly believing a lie,

Ye saw that the land lay fenceless, and ye let the
    months go by
Waiting some easy wonder, hoping some saving
    sign –
Idle – openly idle – in the lee of the forespent Line.
Idle – except for your boasting – and what is your
    boasting worth
If ye grudge a year of service to the lordliest life on
    earth?
Ancient, effortless, ordered, cycle on cycle set,
Life so long untroubled, that ye who inherit forget
It was not made with the mountains, it is not one
    with the deep.
Men, not gods, devised it. Men, not gods, must
    keep.
Men, not children, servants, or kinsfolk called
    from afar,
But each man born in the Island broke to the
    matter of war.
Soberly and by custom taken and trained for the
    same,
Each man born in the Island entered at youth to
    the game –
As it were almost cricket, not to be mastered in
    haste,
But after trial and labour, by temperance, living
    chaste.
As it were almost cricket – as it were even your play,
Weighed and pondered and worshipped, and
    practised day and day.
So ye shall bide sure-guarded when the restless
    lightnings wake
In the womb of the blotting war-cloud, and the
    pallid nations quake.

So, at the haggard trumpets, instant your soul
    shall leap
Forthright, accoutred, accepting – alert from the
    wells of sleep.
So at the threat ye shall summon – so at the need
    ye shall send
Men, not children or servants, tempered and
    taught to the end;
Cleansed of servile panic, slow to dread or despise,
Humble because of knowledge, mighty by
    sacrifice . . .
But ye say, 'It will mar our comfort.' Ye say, 'It
    will minish our trade.'
Do ye wait for the spattered shrapnel ere ye learn
    how a gun is laid?
For the low, red glare to southward when the
    raided coast-towns burn?
(Light ye shall have on that lesson, but little time
    to learn.)
Will ye pitch some white pavilion, and lustily even
    the odds,
With nets and hoops and mallets, with rackets and
    bats and rods?
Will the rabbit war with your foemen – the red
    deer horn them for hire?
Your kept cock-pheasant keep you? – he is master
    of many a shire.
Arid, aloof, incurious, unthinking, unthanking, gelt,
Will ye loose your schools to flout them till their
    browbeat columns melt?
Will ye pray them or preach them, or print them,
    or ballot them back from your shore?
Will your workmen issue a mandate to bid them
    strike no more?

Will ye rise and dethrone your rulers? (Because ye
    were idle both?
Pride by Insolence chastened? Indolence purged
    by Sloth?)
No doubt but ye are the People; who shall make
    you afraid?
Also your gods are many; no doubt but your gods
    shall aid.
Idols of greasy altars built for the body's ease;
Proud little brazen Baals and talking fetishes;
Teraphs of sept and party and wise wood-pavement
    gods –
These shall come down to the battle and snatch
    you from under the rods?
From the gusty, flickering gun-roll with viewless
    salvoes rent,
And the pitted hail of the bullets that tell not
    whence they were sent.
When ye are ringed as with iron, when ye are
    scourged as with whips,
When the meat is yet in your belly, and the boast
    is yet on your lips;
When ye go forth at morning and the noon
    beholds you broke,
Ere ye lie down at even, your remnant, under the
    yoke?

No doubt but ye are the People – absolute, strong, and
    wise;
Whatever your heart has desired ye have not withheld
    from your eyes.
On your own heads, in your own hands, the sin and
    the saving lies!

1902

The Dykes

We have no heart for the fishing – we have no
    hand for the oar –
All that our fathers taught us of old pleases us
    now no more.
All that our own hearts bid us believe we doubt
    where we do not deny –
There is no proof in the bread we eat nor rest
    in the toil we ply.

Look you, our foreshore stretches far through
    sea-gate, dyke, and groin –
Made land all, that our fathers made, where the
    flats and the fairway join.
They forced the sea a sea-league back. They
    died, and their work stood fast.
We were born to peace in the lee of the dykes,
    but the time of our peace is past.

Far off, the full tide clambers and slips,
    mouthing and testing all,
Nipping the flanks of the water-gates, baying
    along the wall;
Turning the shingle, returning the shingle,
    changing the set of the sand . . .
We are too far from the beach, men say, to
    know how the outworks stand.

So we come down, uneasy, to look; uneasily
    pacing the beach.
These are the dykes our fathers made: we have
    never known a breach.
Time and again has the gale blown by and we
    were not afraid;

Now we come only to look at the dykes – at the
    dykes our fathers made.

O'er the marsh where the homesteads cower
    apart the harried sunlight flies,
Shifts and considers, wanes and recovers,
    scatters and sickens and dies –
An evil ember bedded in ash – a spark blown
    west by the wind . . .
We are surrendered to night and the sea – the
    gale and the tide behind!

At the bridge of the lower saltings the cattle
    gather and blare,
Roused by the feet of running men, dazed by
    the lantern-glare.
Unbar and let them away for their lives – the
    levels drown as they stand,
Where the flood-wash forces the sluices aback
    and the ditches deliver inland.

Ninefold deep to the top of the dykes the
    galloping breakers stride,
And their overcarried spray is a sea – a sea on
    the landward side.
Coming, like stallions they paw with their
    hooves, going they snatch with their teeth,
Till the bents and the furze and the sand are
    dragged out, and the old-time hurdles
    beneath.

Bid men gather fuel for fire, the tar, the oil, and
    the tow –
Flame we shall need, not smoke, in the dark if
    the riddled sea-banks go.

Bid the ringers watch in the tower (who knows
      how the dawn shall prove?)
Each with his rope between his feet and the
      trembling bells above.

Now we can only wait till the day, wait and
      apportion our shame.
These are the dykes our fathers left, but we
      would not look to the same.
Time and again were we warned of the dykes,
      time and again we delayed:
Now, it may fall, we have slain our sons, as our
      fathers we have betrayed.

            *   *   *

Walking along the wreck of the dykes, watching
      the work of the seas!
These were the dykes our fathers made to our
      great profit and ease.
But the peace is gone and the profit is gone,
      with the old sure days withdrawn . . .
That our own houses show as strange when we
      come back in the dawn!

1902

The Hyænas

After the burial-parties leave
    And the baffled kites have fled;
The wise hyænas come out at eve
    To take account of our dead.

How he died and why he died
    Troubles them not a whit.
They snout the bushes and stones aside
    And dig till they come to it.

They are only resolute they shall eat
    That they and their mates may thrive,
And they know that the dead are safer meat
    Than the weakest thing alive.

(For a goat may butt, and a worm may sting,
    And a child will sometimes stand;
But a poor dead soldier of the King
    Can never lift a hand.)

They whoop and halloo and scatter the dirt
    Until their tushes white
Take good hold of the Army shirt,
    And tug the corpse to light,

And the pitiful face is shown again
    For an instant ere they close;
But it is not discovered to living men –
    Only to God and to those

Who, being soulless, are free from shame,
    Whatever meat they may find.
Nor do they defile the dead man's name –
    That is reserved for his kind.

The White Man's Burden

The United States and the Philippine Islands

Take up the White Man's burden –
    Send forth the best ye breed –
Go bind your sons to exile
    To serve your captives' need;
To wait in heavy harness
    On fluttered folk and wild –
Your new-caught, sullen peoples,
    Half devil and half child.

Take up the White Man's Burden –
    In patience to abide,
To veil the threat of terror
    And check the show of pride;
By open speech and simple,
    An hundred times made plain,
To seek another's profit,
    And work another's gain.

Take up the White Man's burden –
    The savage wars of peace –
Fill full the mouth of Famine
    And bid the sickness cease;
And when your goal is nearest
    The end for others sought,
Watch Sloth and heathen Folly
    Bring all your hope to nought.

Take up the White Man's burden –
    No tawdry rule of kings,
But toil of serf and sweeper –
    The tale of common things.

The ports ye shall not enter,
    The roads ye shall not tread,
Go make them with your living,
    And mark them with your dead!

Take up the White Man's burden –
    And reap his old reward:
The blame of those ye better,
    The hate of those ye guard –
The cry of hosts ye humour
    (Ah, slowly!) toward the light: –
'Why brought ye us from bondage,
    Our loved Egyptian night?'

Take up the White Man's burden –
    Ye dare not stoop to less –
Nor call too loud on Freedom
    To cloak your weariness;
By all ye cry or whisper,
    By all ye leave or do,
The silent, sullen peoples
    Shall weigh your Gods and you.

Take up the White Man's burden –
    Have done with childish days –
The lightly proffered laurel,
    The easy, ungrudged praise.
Comes now, to search your manhood
    Through all the thankless years,
Cold-edged with dear-bought wisdom,
    The judgment of your peers!

1899

Recessional

God of our fathers, known of old,
    Lord of our far-flung battle-line,
Beneath whose awful Hand we hold
    Dominion over palm and pine –
Lord God of Hosts, be with us yet,
Lest we forget – lest we forget!

The tumult and the shouting dies;
    The Captains and the Kings depart:
Still stands Thine ancient sacrifice,
    An humble and a contrite heart.
Lord God of Hosts, be with us yet,
Lest we forget – lest we forget!

Far-called, our navies melt away;
    On dune and headland sinks the fire:
Lo, all our pomp of yesterday
    Is one with Nineveh and Tyre!
Judge of the Nations, spare us yet,
Lest we forget – lest we forget!

If, drunk with sight of power, we loose
    Wild tongues that have not Thee in awe,
Such boastings as the Gentiles use,
    Or lesser breeds without the Law –
Lord God of Hosts, be with us yet,
Lest we forget – lest we forget!

For heathen heart that puts her trust
    In reeking tube and iron shard,
All valiant dust that builds on dust,
    And guarding, calls not Thee to guard,
For frantic boast and foolish word –
Thy mercy on Thy People, Lord!

1897

'For All We Have and Are'

For all we have and are,
For all our children's fate,
Stand up and take the war.
The Hun is at the gate!
Our world has passed away,
In wantonness o'erthrown.
There is nothing left today
But steel and fire and stone!
    Though all we knew depart,
    The old Commandments stand: –
    'In courage keep your heart,
    In strength lift up your hand.'

Once more we hear the word
That sickened earth of old: –
'No law except the Sword
Unsheathed and uncontrolled.'
Once more it knits mankind,
Once more the nations go
To meet and break and bind
A crazed and driven foe.

Comfort, content, delight,
The ages' slow-bought gain,
They shrivelled in a night.
Only ourselves remain
To face the naked days
In silent fortitude,
Through perils and dismays
Renewed and re-renewed.

Though all we made depart,
The old Commandments stand: –
'In patience keep your heart,
In strength lift up your hand.'

No easy hope or lies
Shall bring us to our goal,
But iron sacrifice
Of body, will, and soul.
There is but one task for all –
One life for each to give.
What stands if Freedom fall?
Who dies if England live?

1914

The Benefactors

Ah! What avails the classic bent
  And what the cultured word,
Against the undoctored incident
  That actually occurred?

And what is Art whereto we press
  Through paint and prose and rhyme –
When Nature in her nakedness
  Defeats us every time?

It is not learning, grace nor gear,
  Nor easy meat and drink,
But bitter pinch of pain and fear
  That makes creation think.

When in this world's unpleasing youth
  Our godlike race began,
The longest arm, the sharpest tooth,
  Gave man control of man;

Till, bruised and bitten to the bone
  And taught by pain and fear,
He learned to deal the far-off stone,
  And poke the long, safe spear.

So tooth and nail were obsolete
  As means against a foe,
Till, bored by uniform defeat,
  Some genius built the bow.

Then stone and javelin proved as vain
  As old-time tooth and nail;
Till, spurred anew by fear and pain,
  Man fashioned coats of mail.

Then was there safety for the rich
  And danger for the poor,
Till someone mixed a powder which
  Redressed the scale once more.

Helmet and armour disappeared
  With sword and bow and pike,
And, when the smoke of battle cleared,
  All men were armed alike . . . .

And when ten million such were slain
  To please one crazy king,
Man, schooled in bulk by fear and pain,
  Grew weary of the thing;

And, at the very hour designed
  To enslave him past recall,
His tooth-stone-arrow-gun-shy mind
  Turned and abolished all.

All Power, each Tyrant, every Mob
  Whose head has grown too large,
Ends by destroying its own job
  And works its own discharge;

And Man, whose mere necessities
  Move all things from his path,
Trembles meanwhile at their decrees,
  And deprecates their wrath!

The Craftsman

Once, after long-drawn revel at the Mermaid,
He to the overbearing Boanerges
Jonson, uttered (if half of it were liquor,
          Blessed be the vintage!)

Saying how, at an alehouse under Cotswold,
He had made sure of his very Cleopatra
Drunk with enormous, salvation-contemning
          Love for a tinker.

How, while he hid from Sir Thomas's keepers,
Crouched in a ditch and drenched by the midnight
Dews, he had listened to gypsy Juliet
          Rail at the dawning.

How at Bankside, a boy drowning kittens
Winced at the business; whereupon his sister –
Lady Macbeth aged seven – thrust 'em under,
          Sombrely scornful.

How on a Sabbath, hushed and compassionate –
She being known since her birth to the townsfolk –
Stratford dredged and delivered from Avon
          Dripping Ophelia.

So, with a thin third finger marrying
Drop to wine-drop domed on the table,
Shakespeare opened his heart till the sunrise
          Entered to hear him.

London waked and he, imperturbable,
Passed from waking to hurry after shadows . . .
Busied upon shows of no earthly importance?
          Yes, but he knew it!

Samuel Pepys

Like as the Oak whose roots descend
  Through earth and stillness seeking food
Most apt to furnish in the end
  That dense, indomitable wood

Which, felled, may arm a seaward flank
  Of Ostia's mole or – bent to frame
The beaked Liburnian's triple bank –
  Carry afar the Roman name;

But which, a tree, the season moves
  Through gentler Gods than Wind or Tide,
Delightedly to harbour doves,
  Or take some clasping vine for bride;

So this man – prescient to ensure
  (Since even now his orders hold)
A little State might ride secure
  At sea from foes her sloth made bold, –

Turned in his midmost harried round,
  As Venus drove or Liber led,
And snatched from any shrine he found
  The Stolen Draught, the Secret Bread.

Nor these alone. His life betrayed
  No gust unslaked, no pleasure missed.
He called the obedient Nine to aid
  The varied chase. And Clio kissed;

Bidding him write each sordid love,
  Shame, panic, stratagem, and lie
In full, that sinners undiscov-
  ered, like ourselves, might say: – ' 'Tis I!'

1933

151

'When 'Omer Smote 'Is Bloomin' Lyre'

When 'Omer smote 'is bloomin' lyre,
   He'd 'eard men sing by land an' sea;
An' what he thought 'e might require,
   'E went an' took – the same as me!

The market-girls an' fishermen,
   The shepherds an' the sailors, too,
They 'eard old songs turn up again,
   But kep' it quiet – same as you!

They knew 'e stole; 'e knew they knowed.
   They didn't tell, nor make a fuss,
But winked at 'Omer down the road,
   An' 'e winked back – the same as us!

Introduction to the 'Barrack-Room Ballads' in
The Seven Seas

Tomlinson

Now Tomlinson gave up the ghost at his house in
    Berkeley Square,
And a Spirit came to his bedside and gripped him
    by the hair –
A Spirit gripped him by the hair and carried him
    far away,
Till he heard as the roar of a rain-fed ford the roar
    of the Milky Way:
Till he heard the roar of the Milky Way die down
    and drone and cease,
And they came to the Gate within the Wall where
    Peter holds the keys.
'Stand up, stand up now, Tomlinson, and answer
    loud and high
The good that ye did for the sake of men or ever
    ye came to die –
The good that ye did for the sake of men on little
    Earth so lone!'
And the naked soul of Tomlinson grew white as a
    rain-washed bone.
'O I have a friend on Earth,' he said, 'that was my
    priest and guide,
And well would he answer all for me if he were at
    my side.'
– 'For that ye strove in neighbour-love it shall be
    written fair,
But now ye wait at Heaven's Gate and not in
    Berkeley Square:
Though we called your friend from his bed this
    night, he could not speak for you,
For the race is run by one and one and never by
    two and two.'

Then Tomlinson looked up and down, and little
    gain was there,
For the naked stars grinned overhead, and he saw
    that his soul was bare.
The Wind that blows between the Worlds, it cut
    him like a knife,
And Tomlinson took up the tale and spoke of his
    good in life.
'O this I have read in a book,' he said, 'and that
    was told to me,
And this I have thought that another man thought
    of a Prince in Muscovy.'
The good souls flocked like homing doves and
    bade him clear the path,
And Peter twirled the jangling Keys in weariness
    and wrath.
'Ye have read, ye have heard, ye have thought,' he
    said, 'and the tale is yet to run:
By the worth of the body that once ye had, give
    answer – what ha' ye done?'
Then Tomlinson looked back and forth, and little
    good it bore,
For the darkness stayed at his shoulder-blade and
    Heaven's Gate before: –
'O this I have felt, and this I have guessed, and
    this I have heard men say,
And this they wrote that another man wrote of a
    carl in Norroway.'
'Ye have read, ye have felt, ye have guessed, good
    lack! Ye have hampered Heaven's Gate;
There's little room between the stars in idleness to
    prate!
For none may reach by hired speech of neighbour,
    priest, and kin

Through borrowed deed to God's good meed that
    lies so fair within;
Get hence, get hence to the Lord of Wrong, for
    the doom has yet to run,
And . . . the faith that ye share with Berkeley
    Square uphold you, Tomlinson!'

         *   *   *

The Spirit gripped him by the hair, and sun by
    sun they fell
Till they came to the belt of Naughty Stars that
    rim the mouth of Hell.
The first are red with pride and wrath, the next
    are white with pain,
But the third are black with clinkered sin that
    cannot burn again.
They may hold their path, they may leave their
    path, with never a soul to mark:
They may burn or freeze, but they must not cease
    in the Scorn of the Outer Dark.
The Wind that blows between the Worlds, it
    nipped him to the bone,
And he yearned to the flare of Hell-gate there as
    the light of his own hearthstone.
The Devil he sat behind the bars, where the
    desperate legions drew,
But he caught the hasting Tomlinson and would
    not let him through.
'Wot ye the price of good pit-coal that I must
    pay?' said he,
'That ye rank yoursel' so fit for Hell and ask no
    leave of me?
I am all o'er-sib to Adam's breed that ye should
    give me scorn,

For I strove with God for your First Father the
    day that he was born.
Sit down, sit down upon the slag, and answer
    loud and high
The harm that ye did to the Sons of Men or ever
    you came to die.'
And Tomlinson looked up and up, and saw
    against the night
The belly of a tortured star blood-red in Hell-
    Mouth light;
And Tomlinson looked down and down, and saw
    beneath his feet
The frontlet of a tortured star milk-white in Hell-
    Mouth heat.
'O I had a love on earth,' said he, 'that kissed me
    to my fall;
And if ye would call my love to me I know she
    would answer all.'
– 'All that ye did in love forbid it shall be written
    fair,
But now ye wait at Hell-Mouth Gate and not in
    Berkeley Square:
Though we whistled your love from her bed
    tonight, I trow she would not run,
For the sin ye do by two and two ye must pay for
    one by one!'
The Wind that blows between the Worlds, it cut
    him like a knife,
And Tomlinson took up the tale and spoke of his
    sins in life: –
'Once I ha' laughed at the power of Love and
    twice at the grip of the Grave,
And thrice I ha' patted my God on the head that
    men might call me brave.'

The Devil he blew on a brandered soul and set it
      aside to cool: –
'Do ye think I would waste my good pit-coal on
      the hide of a brain-sick fool?
I see no worth in the hobnailed mirth or the
      jolthead jest ye did
That I should waken my gentlemen that are
      sleeping three on a grid.'
Then Tomlinson looked back and forth, and there
      was little grace,
For Hell-Gate filled the houseless soul with the
      Fear of Naked Space.
'Nay, this I ha' heard,' quo' Tomlinson, 'and this
      was noised abroad,
And this I ha' got from a Belgian book on the
      word of a dead French lord.'
– 'Ye ha' heard, ye ha' read, ye ha' got, good
      lack! and the tale begins afresh –
Have ye sinned one sin for the pride o' the eye or
      the sinful lust of the flesh?'
Then Tomlinson he gripped the bars and yammered,
      'Let me in –
For I mind that I borrowed my neighbour's wife
      to sin the deadly sin.
The Devil he grinned behind the bars, and banked
      the fires high:
'Did ye read of that sin in a book?' said he; and
      Tomlinson said, 'Ay!'
The Devil he blew upon his nails, and the little
      devils ran,
And he said: 'Go husk this whimpering thief that
      comes in the guise of a man:
Winnow him out 'twixt star and star, and sieve his
      proper worth:

There's sore decline in Adam's line if this be
  spawn of Earth.'
Empusa's crew, so naked-new they may not face
  the fire,
But weep that they bin too small to sin to the
  height of their desire,
Over the coal they chased the Soul, and racked it
  all abroad,
As children rifle a caddis-case or the raven's
  foolish hoard.
And back they came with the tattered Thing, as
  children after play,
And they said: 'The soul that he got from God he
  has bartered clean away.
We have threshed a stook of print and book, and
  winnowed a chattering wind,
And many a soul wherefrom he stole, but his we
  cannot find.
We have handled him, we have dandled him, we
  have seared him to the bone,
And, Sire, if tooth and nail show truth he has no
  soul of his own.'
The Devil he bowed his head on his breast and
  rumbled deep and low: –
'I'm all o'er-sib to Adam's breed that I should bid
  him go.
Yet close we lie, and deep we lie, and if I gave him
  place,
My gentlemen that are so proud would flout me
  to my face;
They'd call my house a common stews and me a
  careless host,
And – I would not anger my gentlemen for the
  sake of a shiftless ghost.'

The Devil he looked at the mangled Soul that
    prayed to feel the flame,
And he thought of Holy Charity, but he thought
    of his own good name: –
'Now ye could haste my coal to waste, and sit ye
    down to fry.
Did ye think of that theft for yourself?' said he;
    and Tomlinson said, 'Ay!'
The Devil he blew an outward breath, for his
    heart was free from care: –
'Ye have scarce the soul of a louse,' he said, 'but
    the roots of sin are there,
And for that sin should ye come in were I the lord
    alone,
But sinful pride has rule inside – ay, mightier than
    my own.
Honour and Wit, fore-damned they sit, to each
    his Priest and Whore;
Nay, scarce I dare myself go there, and you they'd
    torture sore.
Ye are neither spirit nor spirk,' he said; 'ye are
    neither book nor brute –
Go, get ye back to the flesh again for the sake of
    Man's repute.
I'm all o'er-sib to Adam's breed that I should
    mock your pain,
But look that ye win to worthier sin ere ye come
    back again.
Get hence, the hearse is at your door – the grim
    black stallions wait –
They bear your clay to place today. Speed, lest ye
    come too late!
Go back to Earth with a lip unsealed – go back
    with an open eye,

And carry my word to the Sons of Men or ever ye
    come to die:
That the sin they do by two and two they must
    pay for one by one,
And . . . the God that you took from a printed
    book be with you, Tomlinson!'

1891

The Female of the Species

When the Himalayan peasant meets the he-bear in
     his pride,
He shouts to scare the monster, who will often
     turn aside.
But the she-bear thus accosted rends the peasant
     tooth and nail.
For the female of the species is more deadly than
     the male.

When Nag the basking cobra hears the careless
     foot of man,
He will sometimes wriggle sideways and avoid it if
     he can.
But his mate makes no such motion where she
     camps beside the trail.
For the female of the species is more deadly than
     the male.

When the early Jesuit fathers preached to Hurons
     and Choctaws,
They prayed to be delivered from the vengeance
     of the squaws.
'Twas the women, not the warriors, turned those
     stark enthusiasts pale.
For the female of the species is more deadly than
     the male.

Man's timid heart is bursting with the things he
     must not say,
For the Woman that God gave him isn't his to
     give away;

But when hunter meets with husband, each
    confirms the other's tale –
The female of the species is more deadly than the
    male.

Man, a bear in most relations – worm and savage
    otherwise, –
Man propounds negotiations, Man accepts the
    compromise.
Very rarely will he squarely push the logic of a fact
To its ultimate conclusion in unmitigated act.

Fear, or foolishness, impels him, ere he lay the
    wicked low,
To concede some form of trial even to his fiercest
    foe.
Mirth obscene diverts his anger – Doubt and Pity
    oft perplex
Him in dealing with an issue – to the scandal of
    The Sex!

But the Woman that God gave him, every fibre of
    her frame
Proves her launched for one sole issue, armed and
    engined for the same;
And to serve that single issue, lest the generations
    fail,
The female of the species must be deadlier than
    the male.

She who faces Death by torture for each life
    beneath her breast
May not deal in doubt or pity – must not swerve
    for fact or jest.

These be purely male diversions – not in these her
    honour dwells.
She the Other Law we live by, is that Law and
    nothing else.

She can bring no more to living than the powers
    that make her great
As the Mother of the Infant and the Mistress of
    the Mate.
And when Babe and Man are lacking and she
    strides unclaimed to claim
Her right as femme (and baron), her equipment is
    the same.

She is wedded to convictions – in default of
    grosser ties;
Her contentions are her children, Heaven help
    him who denies! –
He will meet no suave discussion, but the instant,
    white-hot, wild,
Wakened female of the species warring as for
    spouse and child.

Unprovoked and awful charges – even so the she-
    bear fights,
Speech that drips, corrodes, and poisons – even so
    the cobra bites,
Scientific vivisection of one nerve till it is raw
And the victim writhes in anguish – like the Jesuit
    with the squaw!

So it comes that Man, the coward, when he
    gathers to confer
With his fellow-braves in council, dare not leave a
    place for her

Where, at war with Life and Conscience, he
    uplifts his erring hands
To some God of Abstract Justice – which no
    woman understands.

And Man knows it! Knows, moreover, that the
    Woman that God gave him
Must command but may not govern – shall
    enthral but not enslave him.
And *She* knows, because She warns him, and Her
    instincts never fail
That the Female of Her Species is more deadly
    than the Male.

1911

The Last Rhyme of True Thomas

The King has called for priest and cup,
  The King has taken spur and blade
To dub True Thomas a belted knight,
  And all for the sake of the songs he made.

They have sought him high, they have sought
    him low,
  They have sought him over down and lea.
They have found him by the milk-white thorn
  That guards the Gates of Faerie.

'Twas bent beneath and blue above:
  Their eyes were held that they might not see
The kine that grazed beneath the knowes,
  Oh, they were the Queens of Faerie!

'Now cease your song,' the King he said,
  'Oh, cease your song and get you dight
To vow your vow and watch your arms,
  For I will dub you a belted knight.

'For I will give you a horse o' pride,
  Wi' blazon and spur and page and squire;
Wi' keep and tail and seizin and law,
  And land to hold at your desire.'

True Thomas smiled above his harp,
  And turned his face to the naked sky,
Where, blown before the wastrel wind,
  The thistledown she floated by.

'I ha' vowed my vow in another place,
  And bitter oath it was on me.
I ha' watched my arms the lee-long night,
  Where five-score fighting men would flee.

'My lance is tipped o' the hammered flame,
  My shield is beat o' the moonlight cold;
And I won my spurs in the Middle World,
  A thousand fathom beneath the mould.

'And what should I make wi' a horse o' pride,
  And what should I make wi' a sword so
    brown,
But spill the rings of the Gentle Folk
  And flyte my kin in the Fairy Town?

'And what should I make wi' blazon and belt,
  Wi' keep and tail and seizin and fee,
And what should I do wi' page and squire
  That am a king in my own countrie?

'For I send east and I send west,
  And I send far as my will may flee,
By dawn and dusk and the drinking rain,
  And syne my Sendings return to me.

'They come wi' news of the groanin' earth,
  They come wi' news of the roarin' sea.
Wi' word of Spirit and Ghost and Flesh,
  And man, that's mazed among the three.'

The King he bit his nether lip,
  And smote his hand upon his knee:

'By the faith of my soul, True Thomas,' he said,
   'Ye waste no wit in courtesie!

'As I desire, unto my pride,
   Can I make Earls by three and three,
To run before and ride behind
   And serve the sons o' my body.'

'And what care I for your row-foot earls,
   Or all the sons o' your body?
Before they win to the Pride o' Name,
   I trow they all ask leave o' me.

'For I make Honour wi' muckle mouth,
   As I make Shame wi' mincing feet,
To sing wi' the priests at the market-cross,
   Or run wi' the dogs in the naked street.

'And some they give me the good red gold,
   And some they give me the white money,
And some they give me a clout o' meal,
   For they be people of low degree.

'And the song I sing for the counted gold
   The same I sing for the white money,
But best I sing for the clout o' meal
   That simple people given me.'

The King cast down a silver groat,
   A silver groat o' Scots money,
'If I come wi' a poor man's dole,' he said,
   'True Thomas, will ye harp to me?'

'Whenas I harp to the children small,
    They press me close on either hand.
And who are you,' True Thomas said,
    That you should ride while they must stand?'

'Light down, light down from your horse o'
        pride,
    I trow ye talk too loud and hie,
And I will make you a triple word,
    And syne, if ye dare, ye shall 'noble me.'

He has lighted down from his horse o' pride,
    And set his back against a stone.
'Now guard you well,' True Thomas said,
    'Ere I rax your heart from your breastbone!'

True Thomas played upon his harp,
    The fairy harp that couldna lee,
And the first least word the proud King heard,
    It harpit the salt tear out o' his e'e.

'Oh, I see the love that I lost long syne,
    I touch the hope that I may not see,
And all that I did of hidden shame,
    Like little snakes they hiss at me.

'The sun is lost at noon – at noon!
    The dread of doom has grippit me.
True Thomas, hide me under your cloak.
    God wot, I'm little fit to dee!'

'Twas bent beneath and blue above –
'Twas open field and running flood –
Where, hot on heath and dyke and wall,
    The high sun warmed the adder's brood.

'Lie down, lie down,' True Thomas said.
  'The God shall judge when all is done,
But I will bring you a better word
  And lift the cloud that I laid on.'

True Thomas played upon his harp,
  That birled and brattled to his hand,
And the next least word True Thomas made,
  It garred the King take horse and brand.

'Oh, I hear the tread o' the fighting-men,
  I see the sun on splent and spear.
I mark the arrow outen the fern
  That flies so low and sings so clear!

'Advance my standards to that war,
  And bid my good knights prick and ride;
The gled shall watch as fierce a fight
  As e'er was fought on the Border-side!'

'Twas bent beneath and blue above,
  'Twas nodding grass and naked sky,
Where, ringing up the wastrel wind,
  The eyass stooped upon the pye.

True Thomas sighed above his harp,
  And turned the song on the midmost string;
And the last least word True Thomas made,
  He harpit his dead youth back to the King.

'Now I am prince, and I do well
  To love my love withouten fear;
To walk with man in fellowship,
  And breathe my horse behind the deer.

'My hounds they bay unto the death,
   The buck has couched beyond the burn,
My love she waits at her window
   To wash my hands when I return.

'For that I live am I content
   (Oh! I have seen my true love's eyes)
To stand with Adam in Eden-glade,
   And run in the woods o' Paradise!'

'Twas naked sky and nodding grass,
   'Twas running flood and wastrel wind,
Where, checked against the open pass,
   The red deer turned to wait the hind.

True Thomas laid his harp away,
   And louted low at the saddle-side;
He has taken stirrup and hauden rein,
   And set the King on his horse o' pride.

'Sleep ye or wake,' True Thomas said,
   'That sit so still, that muse so long?
Sleep ye or wake? – till the Latter Sleep
   I trow ye'll not forget my song.

'I ha' harpit a Shadow out o' the sun
   To stand before your face and cry;
I ha' armed the earth beneath your heel,
   And over your head I ha' dusked the sky.

'I ha' harpit ye up to the Throne o' God,
   I ha' harpit your midmost soul in three.
I ha' harpit ye down to the Hinges o' Hell,
   And – ye – would – make – a Knight o' me!'

1893

Epitaphs of the War

'EQUALITY OF SCARIFICE'

A. 'I was a Have.' B. 'I was a "have-not".'
(*Together.*) 'What hast thou given which I
    gave not?'

A SERVANT

We were together since the War began.
He was my servant – and the better man.

A SON

My son was killed while laughing at some jest.
    I would I knew
What it was, and it might serve me in a time
    when jests are few.

AN ONLY SON

I have slain none except my Mother. She
(Blessing her slayer) died of grief for me.

EX-CLERK

Pity not! The Army gave
Freedom to a timid slave:
In which Freedom did he find
Strength of body, will, and mind:
By which strength he came to prove
Mirth, Companionship, and Love:
For which Love to Death he went:
In which Death he lies content.

THE WONDER

Body and Spirit I surrendered whole
To harsh Instructors – and received a soul . . .
If mortal man could change me through and through
From all I was – what may The God not do?

HINDU SEPOY IN FRANCE

This man in his own country prayed we know
    not to what Powers.
We pray Them to reward him for his bravery in
    ours.

THE COWARD

I could not look on Death, which being known,
Men led me to him, blindfold and alone.

SHOCK

My name, my speech, my self I had forgot.
My wife and children came – I knew them not.
I died. My Mother followed. At her call
And on her bosom I remembered all.

A GRAVE NEAR CAIRO

Gods of the Nile, should this stout fellow here
Get out – get out! He knows not shame nor fear.

PELICANS IN THE WILDERNESS
A Grave near Halfa

The blown sand heaps on me, that none may learn
Where I am laid for whom my children grieve . . .
O wings that beat at dawning, ye return
Out of the desert to your young at eve!

TWO CANADIAN MEMORIALS

1

We giving all gained all.
Neither lament us nor praise.
Only in all things recall,
It is Fear, not Death that slays.

2

From little towns in a far land we came,
To save our honour and a world aflame.
By little towns in a far land we sleep;
And trust that world we won for you to keep!

THE FAVOUR

Death favoured me from the first, well knowing I
  could not endure
    To wait on him day by day. He quitted my
      betters and came
Whistling over the fields, and, when he had made
  all sure,
    'Thy line is at end,' he said, 'but at least I
      have saved its name.'

THE BEGINNER

On the first hour of my first day
  In the front trench I fell.
(Children in boxes at a play
  Stand up to watch it well.)

R.A.F. (AGED EIGHTEEN)

Laughing through clouds, his milk-teeth still
  unshed,

Cities and men he smote from overhead.
His deaths delivered, he returned to play
Childlike, with childish things now put away.

THE REFINED MAN

I was of delicate mind. I stepped aside for
my needs,
Disdaining the common office. I was seen
from afar and killed . . .
How is this matter for mirth? Let each man be
judged by his deeds.
*I have paid my price to live with myself on the
terms that I willed.*

NATIVE WATER-CARRIER (M.E.F.)

Prometheus brought down fire to men.
This brought up water.
The Gods are jealous – now, as then,
Giving no quarter.

BOMBED IN LONDON

On land and sea I strove with anxious care
To escape conscription. It was in the air!

THE SLEEPY SENTINEL

Faithless the watch that I kept: now I have none
to keep.
I was slain because I slept: now I am slain I sleep.
Let no man reproach me again, whatever watch is
unkept –
I sleep because I am slain. They slew me because
I slept.

BATTERIES OUT OF AMMUNITION

If any mourn us in the workshop, say
We died because the shift kept holiday.

COMMON FORM

If any question why we died,
Tell them, because our fathers lied.

A DEAD STATESMAN

I could not dig: I dared not rob:
Therefore I lied to please the mob.
Now all my lies are proved untrue
And I must face the men I slew.
What tale shall serve me here among
Mine angry and defrauded young?

THE REBEL

If I had clamoured at Thy Gate
    For gift of Life on Earth,
And, thrusting through the souls that wait,
    Flung headlong into birth –
Even then, even then, for gin and snare
    About my pathway spread,
Lord, I had mocked Thy thoughtful care
    Before I joined the Dead!
But now? . . . I was beneath Thy Hand
    Ere yet the Planets came.
And now – though Planets pass, I stand
    The witness to Thy shame!

THE OBEDIENT

Daily, though no ears attended,
   Did my prayers arise.
Daily, though no fire descended,
   Did I sacrifice.
Though my darkness did not lift,
   Though I faced no lighter odds,
Though the Gods bestowed no gift,
      None the less,
  None the less, I served the Gods!

A DRIFTER OFF TARENTUM

He from the wind-bitten North with ship and
  companions descended,
   Searching for eggs of death spawned by
   invisible hulls.
Many he found and drew forth. Of a sudden the
  fishery ended
   In flame and a clamorous breath known to
   the eye-pecking gulls.

DESTROYERS IN COLLISION

For Fog and Fate no charm is found
  To lighten or amend.
I, hurrying to my bride, was drowned –
  Cut down by my best friend.

CONVOY ESCORT

I was a shepherd to fools
  Causelessly bold or afraid.
They would not abide by my rules.
  Yet they escaped. For I stayed.

UNKNOWN FEMALE CORPSE

Headless, lacking foot and hand,
Horrible I come to land.
I beseech all women's sons
Know I was a mother once.

RAPED AND REVENGED

One used and butchered me: another spied
Me broken – for which thing an hundred died.
So it was learned among the heathen hosts
How much a freeborn woman's favour costs.

SALONIKAN GRAVE

I have watched a thousand days
Push out and crawl into night
Slowly as tortoises.
Now I, too, follow these.
It is fever, and not the fight –
Time, not battle, – that slays.

THE BRIDEGROOM

Call me not false, beloved,
    If, from thy scarce-known breast
So little time removed,
    In other arms I rest.

For this more ancient bride,
    Whom coldly I embrace,
Was constant at my side
    Before I saw thy face.

Our marriage, often set –
    By miracle delayed –

At last is consummate,
  And cannot be unmade.

Live, then, whom Life shall cure,
  Almost, of Memory,
And leave us to endure
  Its immortality.

V.A.D. (MEDITERRANEAN)

Ah, would swift ships had never been, for then we
  ne'er had found,
These harsh Ægean rocks between, this little
  virgin drowned,
Whom neither spouse nor child shall mourn, but
  men she nursed through pain
And – certain keels for whose return the heathen
  look in vain.

ACTORS

*On a memorial tablet in Holy Trinity Church,
Stratford-on-Avon*

We counterfeited once for your disport
  Men's joy and sorrow: but our day has passed.
We pray you pardon all where we fell short –
  Seeing we were your servants to this last.

JOURNALISTS

*On a panel in the hall of the
Institute of Journalists*

We have served our day.

1914–18

'Bobs'

Field Marshal Lord Roberts of Kandahar:
died in France 1914

There's a little red-faced man,
    Which is Bobs,
Rides the tallest 'orse 'e can –
    Our Bobs.
If it bucks or kicks or rears,
'E can sit for twenty years
With a smile round both 'is ears –
    Can't yer, Bobs?

Then 'ere's to Bobs Bahadur – little Bobs,
    Bobs, Bobs!
'E's our pukka Kandaharder –
    Fightin' Bobs, Bobs, Bobs!
'E's the Dook of *Aggy Chel*;
'E's the man that done us well,
An' we'll follow 'im to 'ell –
    Won't we, Bobs?

If a limber's slipped a trace,
    'Ook on Bobs.
If a marker's lost 'is place,
    Dress by Bobs.
For 'e's eyes all up 'is coat,
An' a bugle in 'is throat,
An' you will not play the goat
    Under Bobs.

'E's a little down on drink,
    Chaplain Bobs;

179

But it keeps us outer Clink –
      Don't it, Bobs?
So we will not complain
Tho' 'e's water on the brain,
If 'e leads us straight again –
      Blue-light Bobs.

If you stood 'im on 'is head,
      Father Bobs,
You could spill a quart of lead
      Outer Bobs.
'E's been at it thirty years,
An-amassin' souveneers
In the way o' slugs an' spears –
      Ain't yer, Bobs?

What 'e does not know o' war,
      Gen'ral Bobs,
You can arst the shop next door –
      Can't they, Bobs?
Oh, 'e's little but he's wise,
'E's terror for 'is size,
An' – 'e – *does* – *not* – *advertise* –
      Do yer, Bobs?

Now they've made a bloomin' Lord
      Outer Bobs,
Which was but 'is fair reward –
      Weren't it, Bobs?
So 'e'll wear a coronet
Where 'is 'elmet used to set;
But we know you won't forget –
      Will yer, Bobs?

Then 'ere's to Bobs Bahadur – little Bobs,
    Bobs, Bobs,
Pocket-Wellin'ton an' *arder* –
      Fightin' Bobs, Bobs, Bobs!
This ain't no bloomin' ode,
But you've 'elped the soldier's load,
An' for benefits bestowed,
      Bless yer, Bobs!

1898

Danny Deever

'What are the bugles blowin' for?' said Files-on-
    Parade.
'To turn you out, to turn you out,' the Colour-
    Sergeant said.
'What makes you look so white, so white?' said
    Files-on-Parade.
'I'm dreadin' what I've got to watch,' the Colour-
    Sergeant said.
    For they're hangin' Danny Deever, you can
        hear the Dead March play,
    The Regiment's in 'ollow square – they're
        hangin' him today;
    They've taken of his buttons off an' cut his
        stripes away,
    An' they're hangin' Danny Deever in the
        mornin'.

'What makes the rear-rank breathe so 'ard?' said
    Files-on-Parade.
'It's bitter cold, it's bitter cold,' the Colour-
    Sergeant said.
'What makes that front-rank man fall down?' said
    Files-on-Parade.
'A touch o' sun, a touch o' sun,' the Colour-
    Sergeant said.
    They are hangin' Danny Deever, they are
        marchin' of 'im round,
    They 'ave 'alted Danny Deever by 'is coffin
        on the ground;
    An' 'e'll swing in 'arf a minute for a sneakin'
        shootin' hound –
    O they're hangin' Danny Deever in the
        mornin'!

' 'Is cot was right-'and cot to mine,' said Files-on-
    Parade.
' 'E's sleepin' out an' far tonight,' the Colour-
    Sergeant said.
'I've drunk 'is beer a score o' times,' said Files-
    on-Parade.
' 'E's drinkin' bitter beer alone,' the Colour-Sergeant
    said.
        They are hangin' Danny Deever, you must
            mark 'im to 'is place,
        For 'e shot a comrade sleepin' – you must
            look 'im in the face;
        Nine 'undred of 'is county an' the Regiment's
            disgrace,
        While they're hangin' Danny Deever in the
            mornin'.

'What's that so black agin the sun?' said Files-on-
    Parade.
'It's Danny fightin' 'ard for life,' the Colour-
    Sergeant said.
'What's that that whimpers over'ead?' said Files-
    on-Parade.
'It's Danny's soul that's passin' now,' the Colour-
    Sergeant said.
        For they're done with Danny Deever, you can
            'ear the quickstep play,
        The Regiment's in column, an' they're
            marchin' us away;
        Ho! the young recruits are shakin', an' they'll
            want their beer today,
        After hangin' Danny Deever in the mornin'!

Tommy

I went into a public 'ouse to get a pint o' beer,
The publican 'e up an' sez, 'We serve no redcoats
here.'
The girls be'ind the bar they laughed an' giggled
fit to die,
I outs into the street again an' to myself sez I:
  O it's Tommy this, an' Tommy that, an'
   'Tommy, go away';
   But it's 'Thank you, Mister Atkins,' when the
    band begins to play –
   The band begins to play, my boys, the band
    begins to play,
   O it's 'Thank you, Mister Atkins,' when the
    band begins to play.

I went into a theatre as sober as could be,
They gave a drunk civilian room, but 'adn't none
for me;
They sent me to the gallery or round the music-
'alls,
But when it comes to fightin', Lord! they'll shove
me in the stalls!
   For it's Tommy this, an' Tommy that, an'
    'Tommy, wait outside';
   But it's 'Special train for Atkins' when the
    trooper's on the tide –
   The troopship's on the tide, my boys, the
    troopship's on the tide,
   O it's 'Special train for Atkins' when the
    trooper's on the tide.

Yes, makin' mock o' uniforms that guard you
    while you sleep
Is cheaper than them uniforms, an' they're
    starvation cheap;
An' hustlin' drunken soldiers when they're goin'
    large a bit
Is five times better business than paradin' in full kit.
      Then it's Tommy this, an' Tommy that, an'
        'Tommy, 'ow's yer soul?'
      But it's 'Thin red line of 'eroes' when the
        drums begin to roll –
      The drums begin to roll, my boys, the drums
        begin to roll,
      O it's 'Thin red line of 'eroes' when the
        drums begin to roll.

We aren't no thin red 'eroes, nor we aren't no
    blackguards too,
But single men in barricks, most remarkable like
    you;
An' if sometimes our conduck isn't all your fancy
    paints,
Why, single men in barricks don't grow into
    plaster saints;
      While it's Tommy this, an' Tommy that, an'
        'Tommy, fall be'ind,'
      But it's 'Please to walk in front, sir,' when
        there's trouble in wind –
      There's trouble in the wind, my boys, there's
        trouble in the wind,
      O it's 'Please to walk in front, sir,' when
        there's trouble in the wind.

You talk o' better food for us, an' schools, an'
    fires, an' all:
We'll wait for extry rations if you treat us rational.
Don't mess about the cook-room slops, but prove
    it to our face
The Widow's Uniform is not the soldier-man's
    disgrace.
    For it's Tommy this, an' Tommy that, an'
        'Chuck him out, the brute!'
    But it's 'Saviour of 'is country' when the guns
        begin to shoot;
    An' it's Tommy this, an' Tommy that, an'
        anything you please;
    An' Tommy ain't a bloomin' fool – you bet
        that Tommy sees!

'Fuzzy-Wuzzy'

Soudan Expeditionary Force. Early Campaigns

We've fought with many men acrost the seas,
An' some of 'em was brave an' some was not:
The Paythan an' the Zulu an' Burmese;
But the Fuzzy was the finest o' the lot.
We never got a ha'porth's change of 'im:
'E squatted in the scrub an' 'ocked our 'orses,
'E cut our sentries up at *Suakim*,
    An' 'e played the cat an' banjo with our forces.
      So 'ere's *to* you, Fuzzy-Wuzzy, at your 'ome
        in the Soudan;
      You're a pore benighted 'eathen but a first-
        class fightin' man;
      We gives you your certificate, an' if you want
        it signed
      We'll come an' 'ave a romp with you whenever
        you're inclined.

We took our chanst among the Kyber 'ills,
The Boers knocked us silly at a mile,
The Burman give us Irriwaddy chills,
An' a Zulu *impi* dished us up in style:
But all we ever got from such as they
Was pop to what the Fuzzy made us swaller;
We 'eld our bloomin' own, the papers say,
But man for man the Fuzzy knocked us 'oller.
      Then 'ere's *to* you, Fuzzy-Wuzzy, an' the
        missis and the kid;
      Our orders was to break you, an' of course we
        went an' did.
      We sloshed you with Martinis, an' it wasn't
        'ardly fair;
      But for all the odds agin' you, Fuzzy-Wuz,
        you broke the square.

'E 'asn't got no papers of 'is own,
'E 'asn't got no medals nor rewards,
So *we* must certify the skill 'e's shown
In usin' of 'is long two-'anded swords:
When 'e's 'oppin' in an' out among the bush
With 'is coffin-'eaded shield an' shovel-spear,
An 'appy day with Fuzzy on the rush
Will last an 'ealthy Tommy for a year.

> So 'ere's *to* you, Fuzzy-Wuzzy, an' your
>   friends which are no more,
> If we 'adn't lost some messmates we would
>   'elp you to deplore.
> But give an' take's the gospel, an' we'll call
>   the bargain fair,
> For if you 'ave lost more than us, you crumpled
>   up the square!

'E rushes at the smoke when we let drive,
An', before we know, 'e's 'ackin' at our 'ead;
'E's all 'ot sand an' ginger when alive,
An' 'e's generally shammin' when 'e's dead.
'E's a daisy, 'e's a ducky, 'e's a lamb!
'E's a injia-rubber idiot on the spree,
'E's the on'y thing that doesn't give a damn
For a Regiment o' British Infantree!

> So 'ere's *to* you, Fuzzy-Wuzzy, at your 'ome
>   in the Soudan;
> You're a pore benighted 'eathen but a first-
>   class fightin' man;
> An' 'ere's *to* you, Fuzzy-Wuzzy, with your
>   'ayrick 'ead of 'air –
> You big black boundin' beggar – for you
>   broke a British square!

Gunga Din

You may talk o' gin and beer
When you're quartered safe out 'ere,
An' you're sent to penny-fights an' Aldershot it;
But when it comes to slaughter
You will do your work on water,
An' you'll lick the bloomin' boots of 'im that's got it.
Now in Injia's sunny clime,
Where I used to spend my time
A-servin' of 'Er Majesty the Queen,
Of all them blackfaced crew
The finest man I knew
Was our regimental bhisti, Gunga Din.
        He was 'Din! Din! Din!
    You limpin' lump o' brick-dust, Gunga Din!
        Hi! Slippy *hitherao*!
        Water, get it! *Panee lao*,
    You squidgy-nosed old idol, Gunga Din.'

The uniform 'e wore
Was nothin' much before,
An' rather less than 'arf o' that be'ind,
For a piece o' twisty rag
An' a goatskin water-bag
Was all the field-equipment 'e could find.
When the sweatin' troop-train lay
In a sidin' through the day,
Where the 'eat would make your bloomin' eyebrows
    crawl,
We shouted 'Harry By!'
Till our throats were bricky-dry,
Then we wopped 'im 'cause 'e couldn't serve us all.

It was 'Din! Din! Din!
You 'eathen, where the mischief 'ave you been?
You put some *juldee* in it
Or I'll *marrow* you this minute
If you don't fill up my helmet, Gunga Din!'

'E would dot an' carry one
Till the longest day was done;
An' 'e didn't seem to know the use o' fear.
If we charged or broke or cut,
You could bet your bloomin' nut,
'E'd be waitin' fifty paces right flank rear.
With 'is mussick on 'is back,
'E would skip with our attack,
An' watch us till the bugles made 'Retire, '
An' for all 'is dirty 'ide
'E was white, clear white, inside
When 'e went to tend the wounded under fire!
It was 'Din! Din! Din!'
With the bullets kickin' dust-spots on the green
When the cartridges ran out,
You could hear the front-ranks shout,
'Hi! ammunition-mules an' Gunga Din!'

I shan't forgit the night
When I dropped be'ind the fight
With a bullet where my belt-plate should 'a' been.
I was chokin' mad with thirst,
An' the man that spied me first
Was our good old grinnin', gruntin' Gunga Din.
'E lifted up my 'ead,
An' he plugged me where I bled,
An' 'e guv me 'arf-a-pint o' water green.

t was crawlin' and it stunk,
But of all the drinks I've drunk,
'm gratefullest to one from Gunga Din.
          It was 'Din! Din! Din!
   'Ere's a beggar with a bullet through 'is spleen;
          'E's chawin' up the ground,
          An' 'e's kickin' all around:
   For Gawd's sake git the water, Gunga Din!'

E carried me away
To where a dooli lay,
An' a bullet come an' drilled the beggar clean.
E put me safe inside,
An' just before 'e died,
'I 'ope you liked your drink,' sez Gunga Din.
So I'll meet 'im later on
At the place where 'e is gone –
Where it's always double drill and no canteen.
E'll be squattin' on the coals
Givin' drink to poor damned souls,
An' I'll get a swig in hell from Gunga Din!
          Yes, Din! Din! Din!
   You Lazarushian-leather Gunga Din!
          Though I've belted you and flayed you,
          By the livin' Gawd that made you,
   You're a better man than I am, Gunga Din!

The Widow at Windsor

'Ave you 'eard o' the Widow at Windsor
　　With a hairy gold crown on 'er 'ead?
She 'as ships on the foam – she 'as millions at 'ome,
　　An' she pays us poor beggars in red.
　　　　(Ow, poor beggars in red!)
There's 'er nick on the cavalry 'orses,
　　There's 'er mark on the medical stores –
An' 'er troopers you'll find with a fair wind be'ind
　　That takes us to various wars.
　　　　(Poor beggars! – barbarious wars!)
　　　　　　Then 'ere's to the Widow at Windsor,
　　　　　　　　An' 'ere's to the stores an' the guns,
　　　　　　The men an' the 'orses what makes up
　　　　　　　　　　　　the forces
　　　　　　O' Missis Victorier's sons.
　　　　　　(Poor beggars! Victorier's sons!)

Walk wide o' the Widow at Windsor,
　　For 'alf o' Creation she owns:
We 'ave bought 'er the same with the sword an'
　　the flame,
An' we've salted it down with our bones.
　　　　(Poor beggars! – it's blue with our bones!)
Hands off o' the sons o' the Widow,
　　Hands off o' the goods in 'er shop,
For the Kings must come down an the Emperors
　　frown
　　When the Widow at Windsor says 'Stop!'
　　　　(Poor beggars! – we're sent to say 'Stop!')
　　　　　　Then 'ere's to the Lodge o' the Widow,
　　　　　　　　From the Pole to the Tropics it runs –

To the Lodge that we tile with the rank
    an' the file,
    An' open in form with the guns.
      (Poor beggars! – it's always they guns!)

We' ave 'eard o' the Widow at Windsor,
    It's safest to leave 'er alone:
For 'er sentries we stand by the sea an' the land
    Wherever the bugles are blown.
      (Poor beggars! – an' don't we get blown!)
Take 'old o' the Wings o' the Mornin',
    An' flop round the earth till you're dead;
But you won't get away from the tune that they
    play
To the bloomin' old rag over'ead.
      (Poor beggars! – it's 'ot over'ead!)
        Then 'ere's to the Sons o' the Widow,
          Wherever, 'owever they roam.
        'Ere's all they desire, an' if they require
          A speedy return to their 'ome.
          (Poor beggars! – they'll never see 'ome!)

The Young British Soldier

When the 'arf-made recruity goes out to the East
'E acts like a babe an' 'e drinks like a beast,
An' 'e wonders because 'e is frequent deceased
 Ere 'e's fit for to serve as a soldier.
  Serve, serve, serve as a soldier,
  Serve, serve, serve as a soldier,
  Serve, serve, serve as a soldier,
   So—oldier *of* the Queen!

Now all you recruities what's drafted today,
You shut up your rag-box an' 'ark to my lay,
An' I'll sing you a soldier as far as I may:
 A soldier what's fit for a soldier.
  Fit, fit, fit for a soldier . . .

First mind you steer clear o' the grog-sellers' huts
 For they sell you Fixed Bay'nets that rots out
  your guts –
Ay, drink that 'ud eat the live steel from your butts
 An' it's bad for the young British soldier.
  Bad, bad, bad for the soldier . . .

When the cholera comes – as it will past a doubt –
Keep out of the wet and don't go on the shout,
For the sickness gets in as the liquor dies out,
 An' it crumples the young British soldier.
  Crum–, crum–, crumples the soldier . . .

But the worst o' your foes is the sun over'ead:
You *must* wear your 'elmet for all that is said:
If 'e finds you uncovered 'e'll knock you down
 dead,
 An' you'll die like a fool of a soldier.
  Fool, fool, fool of a soldier . . .

f you're cast for fatigue by a sergeant unkind,
)on't grouse like a woman nor crack on nor
   blind;
3e handy and civil, and then you will find
   That it's beer for the young British soldier.
      Beer, beer, beer for the soldier . . .

Now, if you must marry, take care she is old –
A troop-sergeant's widow's the nicest, I'm told,
`or beauty won't help if your rations is cold,
   Nor love ain't enough for a soldier.
      'Nough, 'nough, 'nough for a soldier . . .

f the wife should go wrong with a comrade, be
   loth
To shoot when you catch 'em – you'll swing, on
   my oath! –
Make 'im take 'er and keep 'er: that's Hell for
   them both,
   An' you're shut o' the curse of a soldier.
      Curse, curse, curse of a soldier . . .

When first under fire an' you're wishful to duck
)on't look nor take 'eed at the man that is struck.
3e thankful you're livin', and trust to your luck
   And march to your front like a soldier.
      Front, front, front like a soldier . . .

When 'arf of your bullets fly wide in the ditch,
)on't call your Martini a cross-eyed old bitch;
She's human as you are – you treat her as sich,
   An' she'll fight for the young British soldier.
      Fight, fight, fight for the soldier . . .

When shakin' their bustles like ladies so fine,
The guns o' the enemy wheel into line,
Shoot low at the limbers an' don't mind the shine
 For noise never startles the soldier.
   Start–, start–, startles the soldier . . .

If your officer's dead and the sergeants look white,
Remember it's ruin to run from a fight:
So take open order, lie down, and sit tight,
 And wait for supports like a soldier.
   Wait, wait, wait like a soldier . . .

When you're wounded and left on Afghanistan's
 plains,
And the women come out to cut up what remains,
Jest roll to your rifle and blow out your brains
 An' go to your Gawd like a soldier.
  Go, go, go like a soldier,
  Go, go, go like a soldier,
  Go, go, go like a soldier,
   So–oldier of the Queen!

Mandalay

By the old Moulmein Pagoda, lookin' lazy at the
    sea,
There's a Burma girl a-settin', and I know she
    thinks o' me;
For the wind is in the palm-trees, and the temple-
    bells they say:
'Come you back, you British soldier; come you
    back to Mandalay!'
        Come you back to Mandalay,
        Where the old Flotilla lay:
        Can't you 'ear their paddles chunkin'
            from Rangoon to Mandalay?
        On the road to Mandalay,
        Where the flyin'-fishes play,
        An' the dawn comes up like thunder
            outer China 'crost the Bay!

'Er petticoat was yaller an' 'er little cap was green,
An' 'er name was Supi-yaw-lat – jes' the same as
    Theebaw's Queen,
An' I seed her first a-smokin' of a whackin' white
    cheroot,
An' a-wastin' Christian kisses on an 'eathen idol's
    foot:
        Bloomin' idol made o' mud –
        Wot they called the Great Gawd Budd –
        Plucky lot she cared for idols when I
            kissed 'er where she stud!
        On the road to Mandalay . . .

When the mist was on the rice-fields an' the sun
    was droppin' slow,
She'd git 'er little banjo an' she'd sing *'Kulla-lo-lo!'*
With 'er arm upon my shoulder an' 'er cheek agin
    my cheek
We useter watch the steamers an' the *hathis* pilin'
    teak.
        Elephints a-pilin' teak
        In the sludgy, squdgy creek,
        Where the silence 'ung that 'eavy you was
            'arf afraid to speak!
        On the road to Mandalay . . .

But that's all shove be'ind me – long ago an' fur
    away,
An' there ain't no 'buses runnin' from the Bank to
    Mandalay;
An' I'm learnin' 'ere in London what the ten-year
    soldier tells:
'If you've 'eard the East a-callin', you won't never
    'eed naught else.'
        No! you won't 'eed nothin' else
        But them spicy garlic smells,
        An' the sunshine an' the palm-trees an'
            the tinkly temple-bells;
        On the road to Mandalay . . .

I am sick o' wastin' leather on these gritty pavin'-
    stones,
An' the blasted English drizzle wakes the fever in
    my bones;
Tho' I walks with fifty 'ousemaids outer Chelsea
    to the Strand,
An' they talks a lot o' lovin', but wot do they
    understand?

Beefy face an' grubby 'and –
Law! wot do they understand?
I've a neater, sweeter maiden in a cleaner,
    greener land!
On the road to Mandalay . . .

Ship me somewheres east of Suez, where the best
    is like the worst,
Where there aren't no Ten Commandments an' a
    man can raise a thirst;
For the temple-bells are callin', an' it's there that I
    would be –
By the old Moulmein Pagoda, looking lazy at the
    sea;
        On the road to Mandalay,
        Where the old Flotilla lay,
        With our sick beneath the awnings when
            we went to Mandalay!
        On the road to Mandalay,
        Where the flyin'-fishes play,
        An' the dawn comes up like thunder
            outer China 'crost the Bay!

Ford o' Kabul River

Kabul town's by Kabul river –
   Blow the trumpet, draw the sword –
There I lef' my mate for ever,
   Wet an' drippin' by the ford.
      Ford, ford, ford o' Kabul river,
        Ford o' Kabul river in the dark!
      There's the river up and brimmin', an'
        there's 'arf a squadron swimmin'
        'Cross the ford o' Kabul river in the dark.

Kabul town's a blasted place –
   Blow the trumpet, draw the sword –
'Strewth I shan't forget 'is face
   Wet an' drippin' by the ford!
      Ford, ford, ford o' Kabul river,
        Ford o' Kabul river in the dark!
      Keep the crossing-stakes beside you, an' they
        will surely guide you
        'Cross the ford o' Kabul river in the dark.

Kabul town is sun and dust –
   Blow the trumpet, draw the sword –
I'd ha' sooner drownded fust
   'Stead of 'im beside the ford.
      Ford, ford, ford o' Kabul river,
        Ford o' Kabul river in the dark!
      You can 'ear the 'orses threshin'; you can
        'ear the men a-splashin',
        'Cross the ford o' Kabul river in the dark.

Kabul town was ours to take –
  Blow the trumpet, draw the sword –
I'd ha' left it for 'is sake –
  'Im that left me by the ford.
      Ford, ford, ford o' Kabul river,
        Ford o' Kabul river in the dark!
      It's none so bloomin' dry there; ain't you
        never comin' nigh there,
          'Cross the ford o' Kabul river in the dark?

Kabul town'll go to hell –
  Blow the trumpet, draw the sword –
'Fore I see him 'live an' well –
  'Im the best beside the ford.
      Ford, ford, ford o' Kabul river,
        Ford o' Kabul river in the dark!
      Gawd 'elp 'em if they blunder, for their
        boots'll pull 'em under,
          By the ford o' Kabul river in the dark.

Turn your 'orse from Kabul town –
  Blow the trumpet, draw the sword –
'Im an' 'arf my troop is down,
  Down and drownded by the ford.
      Ford, ford, ford o' Kabul river,
        Ford o' Kabul river in the dark!
      There's the river low an' fallin', but it ain't
        no use a-callin'
          'Cross the ford o' Kabul river in the dark!

Gentlemen-Rankers

To the legion of the lost ones, to the cohort of the
    damned,
    To my brethren in their sorrow overseas,
Sings a gentleman of England, cleanly bred,
    machinely crammed,
    And a trooper of the Empress, if you please.
Yes, a trooper of the forces who has run his own
    six horses,
    And faith he went the pace and went it blind,
And the world was more than kin while he held
    the ready tin,
    But today the Sergeant's something less than
        kind.
        We're poor little lambs who've lost our way,
            Baa! Baa! Baa!
        We're little black sheep who've gone astray,
            Baa–aa–aa!
        Gentlemen-rankers out on the spree,
            Damned from here to Eternity,
        God ha' mercy on such as we,
            Baa! Yah! Bah!

Oh, it's sweet to sweat through stables, sweet to
    empty kitchen slops,
    And it's sweet to hear the tales the troopers tell,
To dance with blowzy housemaids at the regimental
    hops
    And thrash the cad who says you waltz too well.
Yes, it makes you cock-a-hoop to be 'Rider' to
    your troop,
    And branded with a blasted worsted spur,
When you envy, O how keenly, one poor Tommy
    living cleanly
    Who blacks your boots and sometimes calls you
        'Sir.'

If the home we never write to, and the oaths we
    never keep,
    And all we know most distant and most dear,
Across the snoring barrack-room return to break
    our sleep,
    Can you blame us if we soak ourselves in beer?
When the drunken comrade mutters and the great
    guard-lantern gutters
    And the horror of our fall is written plain,
Every secret, self-revealing on the aching white-
    washed ceiling,
    Do you wonder that we drug ourselves from
        pain?

We have done with Hope and Honour, we are lost
    to Love and Truth,
    We are dropping down the ladder rung by rung,
And the measure of our torment is the measure of
    our youth.
    God help us, for we knew the worst too young!
Our shame is clean repentance for the crime that
    brought the sentence,
    Our pride it is to know no spur of pride,
And the Curse of Reuben holds us till an alien
    turf enfolds us
    And we die, and none can tell Them where we
        died.
        We're poor little lambs who've lost our way,
            Baa! Baa! Baa!
        We're little black sheep who've gone astray,
            Baa–aa–aa!
        Gentlemen-rankers out on the spree,
        Damned from here to Eternity,
        God ha' mercy on such as we,
            Baa! Yah! Bah!

Private Ortheris's Song

My girl she give me the go onest,
    When I was a London lad;
An' I went on the drink for a fortnight,
    An' then I went to the bad.
The Queen she give me a shillin'
    To fight for 'er over the seas;
But Guv'ment built me a fever-trap,
    An' Injia give me disease.

(*Chorus*)
        Ho! don't you 'eed what a girl says,
           An' don't you go for the beer;
        But I was an ass when I was at grass,
           An' that is why I'm 'ere.

I fired a shot at a Afghan,
    The beggar 'e fired again,
An' I lay on my bed with a 'ole in my 'ed,
    An' missed the next campaign!
I up with my gun at a Burman
    Who carried a bloomin' *dah*,
But the cartridge stuck and the bay'nit bruk,
    An' all I got was the scar.

(*Chorus*)
        Ho! don't you aim at a Afghan,
           When you stand on the skyline clear;
        An' don't you go for a Burman
           If none o' your friends is near.

I served my time for a Corp'ral,
    An' wetted my stripes with pop,

For I went on the bend with a intimate friend,
   An' finished the night in the 'shop'.
I served my time for a Sergeant;
    The Colonel 'e sez 'No!
The most you'll see is a full C.B.'
   An' . . . very next night 'twas so!

(*Chorus*)

      Ho! don't you go for a Corp'ral
        Unless your 'ed is clear;
      But I was an ass when I was at grass,
        An' that is why I'm 'ere.

I've tasted the luck o' the Army
   In barrack an' camp an' clink,
An' I lost my tip through the bloomin' trip
   Along o' the women an' drink.
I'm down at the heel o' my service,
   An' when I am laid on the shelf,
My very worst friend from beginning to end
   By the blood of a mouse was myself!

(*Chorus*)

      Ho! don't you 'eed what a girl says,
        An' don't you go for the beer;
      But I was an ass when I was at grass,
        An' that is why I'm 'ere!

         'The Courting of Dinah Shadd'
         from *Life's Handicap*

Shillin' a Day

My name is O'Kelly, I've heard the Revelly
From Birr to Bareilly, from Leeds to Lahore,
Hong-Kong and Peshawur,
Lucknow and Etawah,
And fifty-five more all endin' in 'pore.'
Black Death and his quickness, the depth and the
    thickness
Of sorrow and sickness I've known on my way,
But I'm old and I'm nervis,
I'm cast from the Service,
And all I deserve is a shillin' a day.
  (Chorus)   Shillin' a day,
               Bloomin' good pay –
               Lucky to touch it, a shillin' a day!

Oh, it drives me half crazy to think of the days I
Went slap for the Ghazi, my sword at my side,
When we rode Hell-for-leather
Both squadrons together,
That didn't care whether we lived or we died.
But it's no use despairin', my wife must go charin'
An' me commissairin', the pay-bills to better,
So if me you be'old
In the wet and the cold,
By the Grand Metropold, won't you give me a letter?
  (Full chorus)   Give 'im a letter –
               'Can't do no better,
               Late Troop-Sergeant-Major an' –
                   runs with a letter!
               Think what 'e 's been,
               Think what 'e 's seen.
               Think of his pension an'
               GAWD SAVE THE QUEEN!

'Back to the Army Again'

I'm 'ere in a ticky ulster an' a broken billycock 'at,
A-layin' on to the sergeant I don't know a gun
    from a bat;
My shirt's doin' duty for jacket, my sock's stickin'
    out o' my boots,
An' I'm learnin' the damned old goose-step along
    o' the new recruits!

    Back to the Army again, sergeant,
      Back to the Army again.
    Don't look so 'ard, for I 'aven't no card,
    I'm back to the Army again!

I done my six years' service. 'Er Majesty sez:
    'Good day –
You'll please to come when you're rung for, an'
    'ere 's your 'ole back-pay;
An' fourpence a day for baccy – an' bloomin'
    gen'rous, too;
An' now you can make your fortune – the same as
    your orf'cers do.'

    Back to the Army again, sergeant,
      Back to the Army again.
    'Ow did I learn to do right-about-turn?
    I'm back to the Army again!

A man o' four-an'-twenty that 'asn't learned of a
    trade –
Beside 'Reserve' agin' him – 'e 'd better be never
    made.
I tried my luck for a quarter, an' that was enough
    for me,
An' I thought of 'Er Majesty's barricks, an' I
    thought I'd go an' see.

> Back to the Army again, sergeant,
> > Back to the Army again.
> 'Tisn 't my fault if I dress when I 'alt –
> > I'm back to the Army again!

The sergeant arst no questions, but 'e winked the
> other eye,
'E sez to me, ''Shun!' an' I shunted, the same as
> in days gone by;
For 'e saw the set o' my shoulders, an' I couldn't
> 'elp 'oldin ' straight
When me an' the other rookies come under the
> barrick-gate.

> > Back to the Army again, sergeant,
> > > Back to the Army again.
> > 'Oo would ha' thought I could carry an'
> > > port?
> > I'm back to the Army again!

I took my bath, an' I wallered – for, Gawd, I
> needed it so!
I smelt the smell o' the barricks, I 'eard the bugles
> go.
I 'eard the feet on the gravel – the feet o' the men
> what drill –
An' I sez to my flutterin' 'eart-strings, I sez to
> 'em, 'Peace, be still!'

> > Back to the Army again, sergeant,
> > > Back to the Army again.
> > 'Oo said I knew when the troopship was
> > > due?
> > I'm back to the Army again!

I carried my slops to the tailor; I sez to 'im, 'None
    o' your lip!
You tight 'em over the shoulders, an' loose 'em
    over the 'ip,
For the set o' the tunic's 'orrid.' An' 'e sez to me,
    'Strike me dead,
But I thought you was used to the business!' an'
    so 'e done what I said.

      Back to the Army again, sergeant,
        Back to the Army again.
      Rather too free with my fancies? Wot – me?
      I'm back to the Army again!

Next week I'll 'ave 'em fitted; I'll buy me a
    swagger-cane;
They'll let me free o' the barricks to walk on the
    Hoe again,
In the name o' William Parsons, that used to be
    Edward Clay,
An' – any pore beggar that wants it can draw my
    fourpence a day!

      Back to the Army again, sergeant,
        Back to the Army again.
      Out o' the cold an' the rain, sergeant,
        Out o' the cold an' the rain.
                'Oo 's there?

    A man that's too good to be lost you,
      A man that is 'andled an' made –
    A man that will pay what 'e cost you
      In learnin' the others their trade – parade!
    You're droppin' the pick o' the Army
      Because you don't 'elp 'em remain,
    But drives 'em to cheat to get out o' the street
      An' back to the Army again!

'Soldier an' Sailor Too'

The Royal Regiment of Marines

As I was spittin' into the Ditch aboard o' the
    Crocodile,
I seed a man on a man-o'-war got up in the
    Reg'lars' style.
'E was scrapin' the paint from off of 'er plates, an'
    I sez to 'im, ' 'Oo are you?'
Sez 'e, 'I'm a Jolly – 'Er Majesty's Jolly – soldier
    an' sailor too!'
'Now 'is work begins by Gawd knows when, and
    'is work is never through;
'E isn't one o' the reg'lar Line, nor 'e isn't one of
    the crew.
'E's a kind of a giddy harumfrodite – soldier an'
    sailor too!

An', after, I met 'im all over the world, a-doin' all
    kinds of things,
Like landin' 'isself with a Gatlin' gun to talk to
    them 'eathen kings;
'E sleeps in an 'ammick instead of a cot, an' 'e
    drills with the deck on a slew,
An' 'e sweats like a Jolly – 'Er Majesty's Jolly –
    soldier an' sailor too!
For there isn't a job on the top o' the earth the
    beggar don't know, nor do –
You can leave 'im at night on a bald man's 'ead,
    to paddle 'is own canoe –
'E 's a sort of a bloomin' cosmopolouse – soldier
    an' sailor too.

We've fought 'em in trooper, we've fought 'em in
    dock, and drunk with 'em in betweens,
When they called us the seasick scull'ry-maids, an'
    we called 'em the Ass-Marines;
But, when we was down for a double fatigue, from
    Woolwich to Bernardmyo,
We sent for the Jollies – 'Er Majesty's Jollies –
    soldier an' sailor too!
They think for 'emselves, an' they steal for
    'emselves, and they never ask what's to do,
But they're camped an' fed an' they're up an' fed
    before our bugle's blew.
Ho! they ain't no limpin' procrastitutes – soldier
    an' sailor too.

You may say we are fond of an 'arness-cut, or
    'ootin ' in barrick-yards,
Or startin' a Board School mutiny along o' the
    Onion Guards;
But once in a while we can finish in style for the
    ends of the earth to view,
The same as the Jollies – 'Er Majesty's Jollies –
    soldier an' sailor too!
They come of our lot, they was brothers to us;
    they was beggars we'd met an' knew;
Yes, barrin' an inch in the chest an' the arm, they
    was doubles o' me an' you;
For they weren't no special chrysanthemums –
    soldier an' sailor too!

To take your chance in the thick of a rush, with
    firing all about,
Is nothing so bad when you've cover to 'and, an'
    leave an' likin' to shout;

But to stand an' be still to the *Birken' ead* drill is a
 damn' tough bullet to chew,
An' they done it, the Jollies – 'Er Majesty's Jollies
 – soldier an' sailor too!
Their work was done when it 'adn 't begun; they
 was younger nor me an' you;
Their choice it was plain between drownin' in
 eaps an' bein' mopped by the screw,
So they stood an' was still to the *Birken'ead* drill,
 soldier an' sailor too!

We're most of us liars, we're 'arf of us thieves, an'
 the rest are as rank as can be,
But once in a while we can finish in style (which I
 'ope it won't 'appen to me).
But it makes you think better o' you an' your
 friends, an' the work you may 'ave to do,
When you think o' the sinkin' *Victorier's* Jollies –
 soldier an' sailor too!
Now there isn't no room for to say ye don't know
 – they 'ave proved it plain and true –
That, whether it's Widow, or whether it's ship,
 Victorier's work is to do,
An' they done it, the Jollies – 'Er Majesty's Jollies
 – soldier an' sailor too!

Sappers

Royal Engineers

When the Waters were dried an' the Earth did
   appear,
   ('It's all one,' says the Sapper),
The Lord He created the Engineer,
   Her Majesty's Royal Engineer,
   With the rank and pay of a Sapper!

When the Flood come along for an extra monsoon,
'Twas Noah constructed the first pontoon
   To the plans of Her Majesty's, etc.

But after fatigue in the wet an' the sun,
Old Noah got drunk, which he wouldn't ha' done
   If he'd trained with, etc.

When the Tower o' Babel had mixed up men's *bat*,
Some clever civilian was managing that,
   An' none of, etc.

When the Jews had a fight at th e foot of a hill,
Young Joshua ordered the sun to stand still,
   For he was a Captain of Engineers, etc.

When the Children of Israel made bricks without
   straw,
They were learnin' the regular work of our Corps,
   The work of, etc.

For ever since then, if a war they would wage,
Behold us a-shinin' on history's page –
   First page for, etc.

213

We lay down their sidings an' help 'em entrain,
An' we sweep up their mess through the bloomin'
  campaign
    In the style of, etc.

They send us in front with a fuse an' a mine
To blow up the gates that are rushed by the Line,
    But bent by, etc.

They send us behind with a pick an' a spade,
To dig for the guns of a bullock-brigade
    Which has asked for, etc.

We work under escort in trousers and shirt,
An' the heathen they plug us tail-up in the dirt,
    Annoying, etc.

We blast out the rock an' we shovel the mud,
We make 'em good roads an' – they roll down the
  khud,
    Reporting, etc.

We make 'em their bridges, their wells, an' their
  huts,
An' the telegraph-wire the enemy cuts,
    An' it's blamed on, etc.

An' when we return, an' from war we would cease,
They grudge us adornin' the billets of peace,
    Which are kept for, etc.

We build 'em nice barracks – they swear they are
  bad
That our Colonels are Methodist, married or mad,
    Insultin', etc.

They haven't no manners nor gratitude too,
For the more that we help 'em, the less will they do,
But mock at, etc.

Now the Line's but a man with a gun in his hand,
An' Cavalry's only what horses can stand,
When helped by, etc.

Artillery moves by the leave o' the ground,
But *we* are the men that do something all round,
For *we* are, etc.

I have stated it plain, an' my argument's thus
('It's all one,' says the Sapper)
There's only one Corps which is perfect – that's us;
An' they call us Her Majesty's Engineers,
Her Majesty's Royal Engineers,
With the rank and pay of a Sapper!

That Day

It got beyond all orders an' it got beyond all 'ope;
    It got to shammin' wounded an' retirin' from
        the 'alt.
'Ole companies was lookin' for the nearest road to
    slope;
    It were just a bloomin' knock-out – an' our fault

    Now there ain't no chorus 'ere to give,
      Nor there ain't no band to play;
    An' I wish I was dead 'fore I done what I did,
      Or seen what I seed that day!

We was sick o' bein' punished, an' we let 'em
    know it, too;
    An' a company-commander up an' 'it us with a
      sword,
An' some one shouted ' 'Ook it!' an' it come to
    sove-ki-poo,
    An' we chucked our rifles from us – O my Gawd!

There was thirty dead an' wounded on the ground
    we wouldn't keep –
    No, there wasn't more than twenty when the
      front begun to go –
But, Christ! along the line o' flight they cut us up
    like sheep,
    An' that was all we gained by doin' so!

I 'eard the knives be'ind me, but I dursn't face my
    man,
    Nor I don't know where I went to, 'cause I didn't
      'alt to see,

Till I 'eard a beggar squealin' out for quarter as 'e
    ran,
    An' I thought I knew the voice an' – it was me!

We was 'idin' under bedsteads more than 'arf a
    march away:
    We was lyin' up like rabbits all about the
      countryside;
An' the Major cursed 'is Maker 'cause 'e'd lived
    to see that day,
    An' the Colonel broke 'is sword acrost, an' cried.

We was rotten 'fore we started – we was never
    disci*plined*;
    We made it out a favour if an order was obeyed.
Yes, every little drummer 'ad 'is rights an' wrongs
    to mind,
    So we had to pay for teachin' – an' we paid!

The papers 'id it 'andsome, but you know the
    Army knows;
    We was put to groomin' camels till the regiments
      withdrew.
An' they gave us each a medal for subduin'
    England's foes,
    An' I 'ope you like my song – because it's true!

> *An' there ain't no chorus 'ere to give,*
>   *Nor there ain't no band to play;*
> *But I wish I was dead 'fore I done what I did,*
>   *Or seen what I seed that day!*

'The Men that Fought at Minden'

In the Lodge of Instruction

The men that fought at Minden, they was rookies
in their time –
    So was them that fought at Waterloo!
All the 'ole command, yuss, from Minden to
Maiwand,
    They was once dam' sweeps like you!

> *Then do not be discouraged, 'Eaven is your 'elper,*
>   *We'll learn you not to forget;*
> *An' you mustn't swear an' curse, or you'll only*
>   *catch it worse,*
>   *For we'll make you soldiers yet!*

The men that fought at Minden, they 'ad stocks
beneath their chins,
    Six inch 'igh an' more;
But fatigue it was their pride, and they *would* not
be denied
    To clean the cook 'ouse floor.

The men that fought at Minden, they had anarchist
bombs
    Served to 'em by name of 'and-grenades;
But they got it in the eye (same as you will by an' by)
    When they clubbed their field-parades.

The men that fought at Minden, they 'ad buttons
up an' down,
    Two-an'-twenty dozen of 'em told;
But they didn't grouse an' shirk at an hour's extry
work,
    They kept 'em bright as gold.

The men that fought at Minden, they was armed
    with musketoons,
        Also, they was drilled by 'alberdiers.
don't know what they were, but the sergeants
    took good care
        They washed be'ind their ears.

The men that fought at Minden, they'ad ever cash
    in 'and
        Which they did not bank nor save,
But spent it gay an' free on their betters – such
    as me –
        For the good advice I gave.

The men that fought at Minden, they was civil –
    yuss, they was –
        Never didn't talk o' rights an' wrongs,
But they got it with the toe (same as you will get
    it – so!) –
        For interrupting songs.

The men that fought at Minden, they was several
    other things
        Which I don't remember clear;
But *that's* the reason why, now the six-year men
    are dry,
        The rooks will stand the beer!

    Then do not be discouraged, 'Eaven is your
        'elper,
        We'll learn you not to forget.
    An' you mustn't swear an' curse, or you'll only
        catch it worse,
            An' we'll make you soldiers yet!

    Soldiers yet, if you've got it in you –

All for the sake of the Core;
Soldiers yet, if we 'ave to skin you –
Run an' get the beer, Johnny Raw – Johnny Raw
Ho! run an' get the beer, Johnny Raw!

The Ladies

I've taken my fun where I've found it;
   I've rogued an' I've ranged in my time;
I've 'ad my pickin' o' sweethearts,
   An' four o' the lot was prime.
One was an 'arf-caste widow,
   One was a woman at Prome,
One was the wife of a *jemadar-sais*,
   An' one is a girl at 'ome.

Now I aren't no 'and with the ladies,
   For, takin' 'em all along,
You never can say till you've tried 'em,
   An' then you are like to be wrong.
There's times when you'll think that you mightn't,
   There's times when you'll know that you might;
But the things you will learn from the Yellow an'
    Brown,
   They'll 'elp you a lot with the White!

I was a young un at 'Oogli,
   Shy as a girl to begin;
Aggie de Castrer she made me,
   An' Aggie was clever as sin;
Older than me, but my first un –
   More like a mother she were –
Showed me the way to promotion an' pay,
   An' I learned about women from 'er!

Then I was ordered to Burma,
   Actin' in charge o' Bazar,
An' I got me a tiddy live 'eathen
   Through buyin' supplies off 'er pa.

Funny an' yellow an' faithful –
    Doll in a teacup she were –
But we lived on the square, like a true-married
    pair,
    An' I learned about women from 'er!

Then we was shifted to Neemuch
    (Or I might ha' been keepin' 'er now),
An' I took with a shiny she-devil,
    The wife of a nigger at Mhow;
'Taught me the gypsy-folks' *bolee*;
    Kind o' volcano she were,
For she knifed me one night 'cause I wished she
    was white,
    And I learned about women from 'er!

Then I come 'ome in a trooper,
    'Long of a kid o' sixteen –
'Girl from a convent at Meerut,
    The straightest I ever 'ave seen.
Love at first sight was 'er trouble,
    She didn't know what it were;
An' I wouldn't do such, 'cause I liked 'er too much,
    But – I learned about women from 'er!

I've taken my fun where I've found it,
    An' now I must pay for my fun,
For the more you 'ave known o' the others
    The less will you settle to one;
An' the end of it's sittin' and thinkin',
    An' dreamin' Hell-fires to see;
So be warned by my lot (which I know you will
    not),
    An' learn about women from me!

What did the Colonel's Lady think?
  Nobody never knew.
Somebody asked the Sergeant's Wife,
  An' she told 'em true!
When you get to a man in the case,
  They're like as a row of pins —
For the Colonel's Lady an' Judy O'Grady
  Are sisters under their skins!

The Sergeant's Weddin'

'E was warned agin 'er –
  That's what made 'im look;
She was warned agin' 'im –
  That is why she took.
'Wouldn't 'ear no reason,
  'Went an' done it blind;
We know all about 'em,
  They've got all to find

Cheer for the Sergeant's weddin' –
  Give 'em one cheer more!
Grey gun-'orses in the lando,
  An' a rogue is married to, etc.

What's the use o' tellin'
  'Arf the lot she's been?
'E's a bloomin' robber,
  An' 'e keeps canteen.
'Ow did 'e get 'is buggy?
  Gawd, you needn't ask!
'Made 'is forty gallon
  Out of every cask!

Watch 'im, with 'is 'air cut,
  Count us filin' by –
Won't the Colonel praise 'is
  Pop–u–lar–i–ty!
We 'ave scores to settle –
  Scores for more than beer;
She's the girl to pay 'em –
  That is why we're 'ere!

See the Chaplain thinkin'?
  See the women smile?
Twig the married winkin'
  As they take the aisle?
Keep your side-arms quiet,
  Dressin' by the Band.
Ho! You 'oly beggars,
  Cough be'ind your 'and!

Now it's done an' over,
  'Ear the organ squeak,
' '*Voice that breathed o'er Eden*' –
  Ain't she got the cheek!
White an' laylock ribbons,
  'Think yourself so fine!
I'd pray Gawd to take yer
  'Fore I made yer mine!

Escort to the kerridge,
  Wish 'im luck, the brute!
Chuck the slippers after –
  (Pity 'tain't a boot!)
Bowin' like a lady,
  Blushin' like a lad –
'Oo would say to see 'em
  Both is rotten bad?

Cheer for the Sergeant's weddin' –
  Give 'em one cheer more!
Grey gun-'orses in the lando,
  An' a rogue is married to, etc.

The 'Eathen

The 'eathen in 'is blindness bows down to wood
    an' stone;
'E don't obey no orders unless they is 'is own;
'E keeps 'is side-arms awful: 'e leaves 'em all
    about,
An' then comes up the Regiment an' pokes the
    'eathen out.

> *All along o' dirtiness, all along o' mess,*
> *All along o' doin' things rather-more-or-less,*
> *All along of abby-nay, kul, an' hazar-ho,*
> *Mind you keep your rifle an' yourself jus' so!*

The young recruit is 'aughty – 'e draf's from Gawd
    knows where;
They bid 'im show 'is stockin's an' lay 'is mattress
    square;
'E calls it bloomin' nonsense – 'e doesn't know, no
    more –
An' then up comes 'is Company an' kicks 'im
    round the floor!

The young recruit is 'ammered – 'e takes it very
    hard;
'E 'angs 'is 'ead an' mutters – 'e sulks about the
    yard;
'E talks o' 'cruel tyrants' which 'e'll swing for by
    an' by,
An' the others 'ears an' mocks 'im, an' the boy
    goes orf to cry.

The young recruit is silly – 'e thinks o' suicide.
'E's lost 'is gutter-devil; 'e 'asn't got 'is pride;
But day by day they kicks 'im, which 'elps 'im on
    a bit,
Till 'e finds 'isself one mornin' with a full an'
    proper kit.

> *Gettin' clear o' dirtiness, gettin' done with mess,*
> *Gettin' shut o' doin' things rather-more-or-less;*
> *Not so fond of abby-nay, kul, nor hazar-ho,*
> *Learns to keep 'is rifle an' 'isself jus' so!*

The young recruit is 'appy – 'e throws a chest to
    suit;
You see 'im grow mustaches; you 'ear 'im slap 'is
    boot.
'E learns to drop the 'bloodies' from every word 'e
    slings,
An' 'e shows an 'ealthy brisket when 'e strips for
    bars an' rings.

The cruel-tyrant-sergeants they watch 'im 'arf a year;
They watch 'im with 'is comrades, they watch 'im
    with 'is beer;
They watch 'im with the women at the regimental
    dance,
And the cruel-tyrant-sergeants send 'is name
    along for 'Lance'.

An' now 'e's 'arf o' nothin', an' all a private yet,
'Is room they up an' rags 'im to see what they will
    get.
They rags 'im low an' cunnin', each dirty trick
    they can,
But 'e learns to sweat 'is temper an' 'e learns to
    sweat 'is man.

An', last, a Colour-Sergeant, as such to be
obeyed,
'E schools 'is men at cricket, 'e tells 'em on
parade;
They sees 'im quick an' 'andy, uncommon set an'
smart,
An' so 'e talks to orficers which 'ave the Core at
'eart.

'E learns to do 'is watchin' without it showin'
plain;
'E learns to save a dummy, an' shove 'im straight
again;
'E learns to check a ranker that's buyin' leave to
shirk;
An' 'e learns to make men like 'im so they'll learn
to like their work.

An' when it comes to marchin' he'll see their
socks are right,
An' when it comes to action 'e shows 'em how to
sight.
'E knows their ways of thinkin' and just what's in
their mind;
'E knows when they are takin' on an' when
they've fell be'ind.

'E knows each talkin' corp'ral that leads a squad
astray;
'E feels 'is innards 'eavin', 'is bowels givin' way;
'E sees the blue-white faces all tryin' 'ard to grin,
An' 'e stands an' waits an' suffers till it's time to
cap 'em in.

An' now the hugly bullets come peckin' through
    the dust,
An' no one wants to face 'em, but every beggar
    must;
So, like a man in irons, which isn't glad to go,
They moves 'em off by companies uncommon
    stiff an' slow.

Of all 'is five years' schoolin' they don't remember
    much
Excep' the not retreatin', the step an' keepin'
    touch.
It looks like teachin' wasted when they duck an'
    spread an' 'op –
But if 'e 'adn't learned 'em they'd be all about the
    shop.

An' now it's ' 'Oo goes backward?' an' now it's
    ' 'Oo comes on?'
And now it's 'Get the doolies', an' now the
    Captain's gone;
An' now it's bloody murder, but all the while they
    'ear
'Is voice, the same as barrick-drill, a-shepherdin'
    the rear.

'E's just as sick as they are, 'is 'eart is like to split,
But 'e works 'em, works 'em, works 'em till he
    feels 'em take the bit;
The rest is 'oldin' steady till the watchful bugles
    play,
An' 'e lifts 'em, lifts 'em, lifts 'em through the
    charge that wins the day!

The 'eathen in 'is blindness bows down to wood an'
    stone;
'E don't obey no orders unless they is 'is own.
The 'eathen in 'is blindness must end where 'e began,
But the backbone of the Army is the Non-commissione
    Man!

Keep away from dirtiness – keep away from mess,
Don't get into doin' things rather-more-or-less!
Let's ha' done with abby-nay, kul, and hazar-ho;
Mind you keep your rifle an' yourself jus' so!

The Absent-Minded Beggar

When you've shouted 'Rule Britannia', when
    you've sung 'God save the Queen',
    When you've finished killing Kruger with your
        mouth,
Will you kindly drop a shilling in my little tambourine
    For a gentleman in khaki ordered South?
He's an absent-minded beggar, and his weaknesses
    are great –
    But we and Paul must take him as we find him –
He is out on active service, wiping something off a
    slate –
    And he's left a lot of little things behind him!
Duke's son – cook's son – son of a hundred kings –
    (Fifty thousand horse and foot going to Table
        Bay!)
Each of 'em doing his country's work
    (and who's to look after their things?)
Pass the hat for your credit's sake,
                        and pay – pay – pay!

There are girls he married secret, asking no
    permission to,
    For he knew he wouldn't get it if he did.
There is gas and coals and vittles, and the house-
    rent falling due,
    And it's more than rather likely there's a kid.
There are girls he walked with casual. They'll be
    sorry now he's gone,
    For an absent-minded beggar they will find him,
But it ain't the time for sermons with the winter
    coming on.
    We must help the girl that Tommy's left behind
        him!

Cook's son – Duke's son – son of a belted Earl –
  Son of a Lambeth publican – it's all the same
    today!
Each of 'em doing his country's work
  (and who's to look after the girl?)
Pass the hat for your credit's sake,
                                  and pay – pay – pay!

There are families by thousands, far too proud to
    beg or speak,
  And they'll put their sticks and bedding up the
    spout,
And they'll live on half o' nothing, paid 'em
    punctual once a week,
  'Cause the man that earns the wage is ordered
    out.
He's an absent-minded beggar, but he heard his
    country call,
  And his reg'ment didn't need to send to find
    him!
He chucked his job and joined it – so the job
    before us all
  Is to help the home that Tommy's left behind
    him!
Duke's job – cook's job – gardener, baronet, groom,
  Mews or palace or paper-shop, there's someone
    gone away!
Each of 'em doing his country's work
  (and who's to look after the room?)
Pass the hat for your credit's sake,
                                  and pay – pay – pay!

Let us manage so as, later, we can look him in the
    face,
  And tell him – what he'd very much prefer –

That, while he saved the Empire, his employer
  saved his place,
    And his mates (that's you and me) looked out
      for *her*.
He's an absent-minded beggar and he may forget
  it all,
    But we do not want his kiddies to remind him
That we sent 'em to the workhouse while their
  daddy hammered Paul,
    So we'll help the homes that Tommy left behind
      him!
Cook's home – Duke's home – home of a millionaire,
  (Fifty thousand horse and foot going to Table
    Bay!)
Each of 'em doing his country's work
  (and what have you got to spare?)
Pass the hat for your credit's sake,
                        and pay – pay – pay!

Boots

Infantry Columns

We're foot–slog–slog–slog–sloggin' over Africa –
Foot–foot–foot–foot–sloggin' over Africa –
(Boots–boots–boots–boots–movin' up and down
    again!)
          There's no discharge in the war!

Seven–six–eleven–five–nine-an'-twenty mile today –
Four–eleven–seventeen–thirty-two the day before –
(Boots–boots–boots–boots–movin' up and down
    again!)
          There's no discharge in the war!

Don't–don't–don't–don't–look at what's in front of
    you.
(Boots–boots–boots–boots–movin' up an' down
    again);
Men–men–men–men–men go mad with watchin' 'em,
          An' there's no discharge in the war!

Try–try–try–try–to think o' something different –
Oh–my–God–keep–me from goin' lunatic!
(Boots–boots–boots–boots–movin' up an' down
    again!)
          There's no discharge in the war!

Count–count–count–count–the bullets in the
    bandoliers.
If–your–eyes–drop–they will get atop o' you!
(Boots–boots–boots–boots–movin' up and down
    again)–
          There's no discharge in the war!

We–can–stick–out–'unger, thirst, an' weariness,
But–not–not–not–not the chronic sight of 'em –
Boots–boots–boots–boots–movin' up an' down
again,

> An' there's no discharge in the war!

'Tain't–so–bad–by–day because o' company,
But night–brings–long–strings–o' forty thousand
million
Boots–boots–boots–boots–movin' up an' down
again.

> There's no discharge in the war!

I–'ave–marched–six–weeks in 'Ell an' certify
It–is–not–fire–devils, dark, or anything,
But boots–boots–boots–boots–movin' up an' down
again,

> An' there's no discharge in the war!

The Married Man

Reservist of the Line

The bachelor 'e fights for one
   As joyful as can be;
But the married man don't call it fun,
   Because 'e fights for three –
For 'Im an' 'Er an' It
   (An' Two an' One make Three)
'E wants to finish 'is little bit,
   An' 'e wants to go 'ome to 'is tea!

The bachelor pokes up 'is 'ead
   To see if you are gone;
But the married man lies down instead,
   An' waits till the sights come on,
For 'Im an' 'Er an' a hit
   (Direct or ricochee)
'E wants to finish 'is little bit,
   An' 'e wants to go 'ome to 'is tea.

The bachelor will miss you clear
   To fight another day;
But the married man, 'e says 'No fear!'
   'E wants you out of the way
Of 'Im an' 'Er an' It
   (An' 'is road to 'is farm or the sea),
'E wants to finish 'is little bit,
   An' 'e wants to go 'ome to 'is tea.

The bachelor 'e fights 'is fight
   An' stretches out an' snores;
But the married man sits up all night –

For 'e don't like out-o'-doors.
'E'll strain an' listen an' peer
   An' give the first alarm –
For the sake o' the breathin' 'e's used to 'ear,
   An' the 'ead on the thick of 'is arm.

The bachelor may risk 'is 'ide
   To 'elp you when you're downed;
But the married man will wait beside
   Till the ambulance comes round.
'E'll take your 'ome address
   An' all you've time to say,
Or if 'e sees there's 'ope, 'e'll press
   Your art'ry 'alf the day –

For 'Im an' 'Er an' It
   (An' One from Three leaves Two),
For 'e knows you wanted to finish your bit,
   An' 'e knows 'oo's wantin' you.
Yes, 'Im an' 'Er an' It
   (Our 'oly One in Three),
We're all of us anxious to finish our bit,
   An' we want to get 'ome to our tea!

Yes, It an' 'Er an' 'Im,
   Which often makes me think
The married man must sink or swim
   An' – 'e can't afford to sink!
Oh, 'Im an' It an' 'Er
   Since Adam an' Eve began!
So I'd rather fight with the bacheler
   An' be nursed by the married man!

Stellenbosch

Composite Columns

The General 'eard the firin' on the flank,
  An' 'e sent a mounted man to bring 'im back
The silly, pushin' person's name an' rank
  'Oo'd dared to answer Brother Boer's attack:
For there might 'ave been a serious engagement,
  An' 'e might 'ave wasted 'alf a dozen men;
So 'e ordered 'im to stop 'is operations round the
    kopjes,
  An' 'e told 'im off before the Staff at ten!

      And it all goes into the laundry,
      But it never comes out in the wash,
      'Ow we're sugared about by the old men
      ('Eavy-sterned amateur old men!)
      That 'amper an' 'inder an' scold men
      For fear o' Stellenbosch!

The General 'ad 'produced a great effect,'
  The General 'ad the country cleared – almost;
The General ''ad no reason to expect,'
  And the Boers 'ad us bloomin' well on toast!
For we might 'ave crossed the drift before the
    twilight,
  Instead o' sitting down an' takin' root;
But we was not allowed, so the Boojers scooped
    the crowd,
  To the last survivin' bandolier an' boot.

The General saw the farm'ouse in 'is rear,
  With its stoep so nicely shaded from the sun;

Sez 'e, 'I'll pitch my tabernacle 'ere,'
  An' 'e kept us muckin' round till 'e 'ad done,
For 'e might 'ave caught the confluent pneumonia
  From sleepin' in his gaiters in the dew;
So 'e took a book an' dozed while the other
    columns closed,
  And De Wet's commando out an' trickled through!

The General saw the mountain-range ahead,
  With their 'elios showin' saucy on the 'eight,
So 'e 'eld us to the level ground instead,
  An' telegraphed the Boojers wouldn't fight.
For 'e might 'ave gone an' sprayed 'em with a
    pompom,
  Or 'e might 'ave slung a squadron out to see –
But 'e wasn't takin' chances in them 'igh an'
    'ostile kranzes –
  He was markin' time to earn a K.C.B.

The General got 'is decorations thick
  (The men that backed 'is lies could not complain),
The Staff 'ad D.S.O's till we was sick,
  An' the soldier – 'ad the work to do again!
For 'e might 'ave known the District was an 'otbed,
  Instead of 'andin' over, upside-down,
To a man 'oo 'ad to fight 'alf a year to put it right,
  While the General sat an' slandered 'im in town!

> An' it all went into the laundry,
> But it never came out in the wash.
> We were sugared about by the old men
> (Panicky, perishin' old men)
> That 'amper an' 'inder an' scold men
> For fear o' Stellenbosch!

Ubique

Royal Artillery

There is a word you often see, pronounce it as
    you may –
'You bike', 'you bykwee', 'ubbikwe' – alludin' to
    R.A.
It serves 'Orse, Field, an' Garrison as motto for a
    crest;
An' when you've found out all it means I'll tell
    you 'alf the rest.

Ubique means the long-range Krupp be'ind the
    low-range 'ill –
Ubique means you'll pick it up an', while you do,
    stand still.
Ubique means you've caught the flash an' timed it
    by the sound.
Ubique means five gunners' 'ash before you've
    loosed a round.

Ubique means Blue Fuse, an' make the 'ole to
    sink the trail.
Ubique means stand up an' take the Mauser's 'alf-
    mile 'ail.
Ubique means the crazy team not God nor man
    can 'old.
Ubique means that 'orse's scream which turns
    your innards cold!

Ubique means 'Bank, 'Olborn, Bank – a penny all
    the way' –
The soothin', jingle-bump-an'-clank from day to
    peaceful day.
Ubique means 'They've caught De Wet, an' now
    we shan't be long.'

Ubique means 'I much regret, the beggar's goin'
     strong!'

Ubique means the tearin' drift where, breech-
     blocks jammed with mud,
The khaki muzzles duck an' lift across the khaki
     flood.
Ubique means the dancing plain that changes
     rocks to Boers.
Ubique means mirage again an' shellin' all
     outdoors.

Ubique means 'Entrain at once for Grootdefeat-
     fontein.'
Ubique means 'Off-load your guns' – at midnight
     in the rain!
Ubique means 'More mounted men. Return all
     guns to store.'
Ubique means the R.A.M.R. Infantillery Corps.

Ubique means that warnin' grunt the perished
     linesman knows,
When o'er 'is strung an' sufferin' front the
     shrapnel sprays 'is foes;
An' as their firin' dies away the 'usky whisper runs
From lips that 'aven't drunk all day: 'The Guns!
     Thank Gawd, the Guns!'

Extreme, depressed, point-blank or short, end-
     first or any'ow,
From Colesberg Kop to Quagga's Poort – from
     Ninety-Nine till now –
By what I've 'eard the others tell an' I in spots
     'ave seen,
There's nothin' this side 'Eaven or 'Ell Ubique
     doesn't mean!

'Cities and Thrones and Powers'

Cities and Thrones and Powers
  Stand in Time's eye,
Almost as long as flowers,
  Which daily die:
But, as new buds put forth
  To glad new men,
Out of the spent and unconsidered Earth
  The Cities rise again.

This season's Daffodil,
  She never hears
What change, what chance, what chill,
  Cut down last year's;
But with bold countenance,
  And knowledge small,
Esteems her seven days' continuance
  To be perpetual.

So Time that is o'er-kind
  To all that be,
Ordains us e'en as blind,
  As bold as she:
That in our very death,
  And burial sure,
Shadow to shadow, well persuaded, saith,
  'See how our works endure!'

'A Centurion of the Thirtieth' from
Puck of Pook's Hill

Puck's Song

See you the ferny ride that steals
Into the oak-woods far?
O that was whence they hewed the keels
That rolled to Trafalgar.

And mark you where the ivy clings
To Bayham's mouldering walls?
O there we cast the stout railings
That stand around St Paul's.

See you the dimpled track that runs
All hollow through the wheat?
O that was where they hauled the guns
That smote King Philip's fleet.

(Out of the Weald, the secret Weald,
Men sent in ancient years
The horseshoes red at Flodden Field,
The arrows at Poitiers!)

See you our little mill that clacks,
So busy by the brook?
She has ground her corn and paid her tax
Ever since Domesday Book.

See you our stilly woods of oak,
And the dread ditch beside?
O that was where the Saxons broke
On the day that Harold died.

See you the windy levels spread
About the gates of Rye?
O that was where the Northmen fled,
When Alfred's ships came by.

See you our pastures wide and lone,
Where the red oxen browse?
O there was a City thronged and known,
Ere London boasted a house.

And see you, after rain, the trace
Of mound and ditch and wall?
O that was a Legion's camping-place,
When Caesar sailed from Gaul.

And see you marks that show and fade,
Like shadows on the Downs?
O they are the lines the Flint Men made,
To guard their wondrous towns.

Trackway and Camp and City lost,
Salt Marsh where now is corn –
Old Wars, old Peace, old Arts that cease,
And so was England born!

She is not any common Earth,
Water or wood or air,
But Merlin's Isle of Gramarye,
Where you and I will fare!

Enlarged from *Puck of Pook's Hill*

The Way Through the Woods

They shut the road through the woods
Seventy years ago.
Weather and rain have undone it again,
And now you would never know
There was once a road through the woods
Before they planted the trees.
It is underneath the coppice and heath
And the thin anemones.
Only the keeper sees
That, where the ring-dove broods,
And the badgers roll at ease,
There was once a road through the woods.

Yet, if you enter the woods
Of a summer evening late,
When the night-air cools on the trout-ringed pools
Where the otter whistles his mate,
(They fear not men in the woods,
Because they see so few.)
You will hear the beat of a horse's feet,
And the swish of a skirt in the dew,
Steadily cantering through
The misty solitudes,
As though they perfectly knew
The old lost road through the woods . . .
But there is no road through the woods.

'Marklake Witches' from *Rewards and Fairies*

The Run of the Downs

The Weald is good, the Downs are best –
I'll give you the run of 'em, East to West.
Beachy Head and Winddoor Hill,
They were once and they are still.
Firle, Mount Caburn and Mount Harry
Go back as far as sums'll carry.
Ditchling Beacon and Chanctonbury Ring,
They have looked on many a thing,
And what those two have missed between 'em,
I reckon Truleigh Hill has seen 'em.
Highden, Bignor and Duncton Down
Knew Old England before the Crown.
Linch Down, Treyford and Sunwood
Knew Old England before the Flood;
And when you end on the Hampshire side –
Butser's old as Time and Tide.
The Downs are sheep, the Weald is corn,
You be glad you are Sussex born!

'The Knife and the Naked Chalk' from
Rewards and Fairies

Sir Richard's Song

(A.D. 1066)

I followed my Duke ere I was a lover,
    To take from England fief and fee;
But now this game is the other way over –
    But now England hath taken me!

I had my horse, my shield and banner,
    And a boy's heart, so whole and free;
But now I sing in another manner –
    But now England hath taken me!

As for my Father in his tower,
    Asking news of my ship at sea,
He will remember his own hour –
    Tell him England hath taken me!

As for my Mother in her bower,
    That rules my Father so cunningly,
She will remember a maiden's power –
    Tell her England hath taken me!

As for my Brother in Rouen City,
    A nimble and naughty page is he,
But he will come to suffer and pity –
    Tell him England hath taken me!

As for my little Sister waiting
    In the pleasant orchards of Normandie,
Tell her youth is the time for mating –
    Tell her England hath taken me!

As for my comrades in camp and highway,
　　That lift their eyebrows scornfully,
Tell them their way is not my way –
　　Tell them England hath taken me!

Kings and Princes and Barons famèd,
　　Knights and Captains in your degree;
Hear me a little before I am blamèd –
　　Seeing England hath taken me!

Howso great man's strength be reckoned,
　　There are two things he cannot flee.
Love is the first, and Death is the second –
　　And Love in England hath taken me!

'Young Men at the Manor' from
Puck of Pook's Hill

A Tree Song

(A.D. 1200)

Of all the trees that grow so fair,
    Old England to adorn,
Greater are none beneath the Sun
    Than Oak, and Ash, and Thorn.
Sing Oak, and Ash, and Thorn, good sirs,
    (All of a Midsummer morn!)
Surely we sing no little thing
    In Oak, and Ash, and Thorn!

Oak of the Clay lived many a day
    Or ever Æneas began.
Ash of the Loam was a lady at home
    When Brut was an outlaw man.
Thorn of the Down saw New Troy Town
    (From which was London born);
Witness hereby the ancientry
    Of Oak, and Ash, and Thorn!

Yew that is old in churchyard-mould,
    He breedeth a mighty bow.
Alder for shoes do wise men choose,
    And beech for cups also.
But when ye have killed, and your bowl is
        spilled,
    And your shoes are clean outworn,
Back ye must speed for all that ye need
    To Oak, and Ash, and Thorn!

Ellum she hateth mankind, and waiteth
    Till every gust be laid

To drop a limb on the head of him
  That anyway trusts her shade.
But whether a lad be sober or sad,
  Or mellow with ale from the horn,
He will take no wrong when he lieth along
  'Neath Oak, and Ash, and Thorn!

Oh, do not tell the Priest our plight,
  Or he would call it a sin;
But – we have been out in the woods all night,
  A-conjuring Summer in!
And we bring you news by word of mouth –
  Good news for cattle and corn –
Now is the Sun come up from the South
  With Oak, and Ash, and Thorn!

Sing Oak, and Ash, and Thorn, good sirs
  (All of a Midsummer morn)!
England shall bide till Judgment Tide
  By Oak, and Ash, and Thorn!

  'Weland's Sword' from *Puck of Pook's Hill*

A Charm

Take of English earth as much
As either hand may rightly clutch.
In the taking of it breathe
Prayer for all who lie beneath.
Not the great nor well-bespoke,
But the mere uncounted folk
Of whose life and death is none
Report or lamentation.
   Lay that earth upon thy heart,
   And thy sickness shall depart!

It shall sweeten and make whole
Fevered breath and festered soul.
It shall mightily restrain
Over-busied hand and brain.
It shall ease thy mortal strife
'Gainst the immortal woe of life,
Till thyself, restored, shall prove
By what grace the Heavens do move.

Take of English flowers these –
Spring's full-facèd primroses,
Summer's wild wide-hearted rose,
Autumn's wallflower of the close,
And, thy darkness to illume,
Winter's bee-thronged ivy-bloom.
Seek and serve them where they bide
From Candlemas to Christmas-tide,
   For these simples, used aright,
   Can restore a failing sight.

These shall cleanse and purify
Webbed and inward-turning eye;
These shall show thee treasure hid
Thy familiar fields amid;
And reveal (which is thy need)
Every man a King indeed!

Introduction to *Rewards and Fairies*

Cold Iron

'Gold is for the mistress – silver for the maid –
Copper for the craftsman cunning at his trade.'
'Good!' said the Baron, sitting in his hall,
'But Iron – Cold Iron – is master of them all.'

So he made rebellion 'gainst the King his liege,
Camped before his citadel and summoned it to
      siege.
'Nay!' said the cannoneer on the castle wall,
'But Iron – Cold Iron – shall be master of you all!'

Woe for the Baron and his knights so strong,
When the cruel cannonballs laid 'em all along;
He was taken prisoner, he was cast in thrall,
And Iron – Cold Iron – was master of it all!

Yet his King spake kindly (ah, how kind a Lord!)
'What if I release thee now and give thee back thy
      sword?'
'Nay!' said the Baron, 'mock not at my fall,
For Iron – Cold Iron – is master of men all.'

'Tears are for the craven, prayers are for the clown –
Halters for the silly neck that cannot keep a crown.'
'As my loss is grievous, so my hope is small,
For Iron – Cold Iron – must be master of men all!'

Yet his King made answer (few such Kings there
      be!)
'Here is Bread and here is Wine – sit and sup with
      me.
Eat and drink in Mary's Name, the whiles I do
      recall

How Iron – Cold Iron – can be master of men all!

He took the Wine and blessed it. He blessed and
        brake the Bread.
With His own Hands He served Them, and
        presently He said:
'See! These Hands they pierced with nails, outside
        My city wall,
Show Iron – Cold Iron – to be master of men all.

'Wounds are for the desperate, blows are for the
        strong.
Balm and oil for weary hearts all cut and bruised
        with wrong.
I forgive thy treason – I redeem thy fall –
For Iron – Cold Iron – must be master of men
        all!'

'Crowns are for the valiant – sceptres for the bold!
Thrones and powers for mighty men who dare to take
        and hold!'
'Nay!' said the Baron, kneeling in his hall,
'But Iron – Cold Iron – is master of men all!
Iron out of Calvary is master of men all!'

'Cold Iron' from *Rewards and Fairies*

Eddi's Service

(A.D. 687)

Eddi, priest of St Wilfrid
  In his chapel at Manhood End,
Ordered a midnight service
  For such as cared to attend.

But the Saxons were keeping Christmas,
  And the night was stormy as well.
Nobody came to service,
  Though Eddi rang the bell.

' 'Wicked weather for walking,'
  Said Eddi of Manhood End.
'But I must go on with the service
  For such as care to attend.'

The altar-lamps were lighted, –
  An old marsh-donkey came,
Bold as a guest invited,
  And stared at the guttering flame.

The storm beat on at the windows,
  The water splashed on the floor,
And a wet, yoke-weary bullock
  Pushed in through the open door.

'How do I know what is greatest,
  How do I know what is least?
That is My Father's business,'
  Said Eddi, Wilfrid's priest.

'But – three are gathered together –
  Listen to me and attend.

255

I bring good news, my brethren!'
  Said Eddi of Manhood End.

And he told the Ox of a Manger
  And a Stall in Bethlehem,
And he spoke to the Ass of a Rider
  That rode to Jerusalem.

They steamed and dripped in the chancel,
  They listened and never stirred,
While, just as though they were Bishops,
  Eddi preached them The Word,

Till the gale blew off on the marshes
  And the windows showed the day,
And the Ox and the Ass together
  Wheeled and clattered away.

And when the Saxons mocked him,
  Said Eddi of Manhood End,
'I dare not shut His chapel
  On such as care to attend.'

'The Conversion of St Wilfrid' from
Rewards and Fairies

The Waster

From the date that the doors of his prep-school close
    On the lonely little son
He is taught by precept, insult, and blows
    The Things that Are Never Done.
Year after year, without favour or fear,
    From seven to twenty-two,
His keepers insist he shall learn the list
    Of the things no fellow can do.
(They are not so strict with the average Pict
    And it isn't set to, etc.)

For this and not for the profit it brings
    Or the good of his fellow-kind
He is and suffers unspeakable things
    In body and soul and mind.
But the net result of that Primitive Cult,
    Whatever else may be won,
Is definite knowledge ere leaving College
    Of the Things that Are Never Done.
(An interdict which is strange to the Pict
    And was never revealed to, etc.)

Slack by training and slow by birth,
    Only quick to despise,
Largely assessing his neighbour's worth
    By the hue of his socks or ties,
A loafer-in-grain, his foes maintain,
    And how shall we combat their view
When, atop of his natural sloth, he holds
    There are Things no Fellow can do?
(Which is why he is licked from the first by the Pict
    And left at the post by, etc.)

1930

257

Harp Song of the Dane Women

What is a woman that you forsake her,
And the hearth-fire and the home-acre,
To go with the old grey Widow-maker?

She has no house to lay a guest in –
But one chill bed for all to rest in,
That the pale suns and the stray bergs nest in.

She has no strong white arms to fold you,
But the ten-times-fingering weed to hold you –
Out on the rocks where the tide has rolled you.

Yet, when the signs of summer thicken,
And the ice breaks, and the birch-buds quicken,
Yearly you turn from our side, and sicken –

Sicken again for the shouts and the slaughters.
You steal away to the lapping waters,
And look at your ship in her winter-quarters.

You forget our mirth, and talk at the tables,
The kine in the shed and the horse in the stables –
To pitch her sides and go over her cables.

Then you drive out where the storm-clouds swallow
And the sound of your oar-blades, falling hollow,
Is all we have left through the months to follow.

Ah, what is Woman that you forsake her,
And the hearth-fire and the home-acre,
To go with the old grey Widow-maker?

'The Knights of the Joyous Venture' from
Puck of Pook's Hill

258

The Winners

'The Story of the Gadsbys'

What is the moral? Who rides may read.
When the night is thick and the tracks are blind
A friend at a pinch is a friend indeed,
But a fool to wait for the laggard behind.
Down to Gehenna or up to the Throne,
He travels the fastest who travels alone.

White hands cling to the tightened rein,
Slipping the spur from the booted heel,
Tenderest voices cry 'Turn again!'
Red lips tarnish the scabbarded steel.
High hopes faint on a warm hearthstone –
He travels the fastest who travels alone.

One may fall but he falls by himself –
Falls by himself with himself to blame.
One may attain and to him is pelf –
Loot of the city in Gold or Fame.
Plunder of earth shall be all his own
Who travels the fastest and travels alone.

Wherefore the more ye be holpen and stayed,
Stayed by a friend in the hour of toil,
Sing the heretical song I have made –
His be the labour and yours be the spoil.
Win by his aid and the aid disown –
He travels the fastest who travels alone!

The Law of the Jungle

Now this is the Law of the Jungle – as old and as true
*   as the sky;*
And the Wolf that shall keep it may prosper, but the
*   Wolf that shall break it must die.*

As the creeper that girdles the tree-trunk the Law
*   runneth forward and back –*
For the strength of the Pack is the Wolf, and the
*   strength of the Wolf is the Pack.*

Wash daily from nose-tip to tail-tip; drink deeply,
    but never too deep;
And remember the night is for hunting, and forget
    not the day is for sleep.

The Jackal may follow the Tiger, but, Cub, when
    thy whiskers are grown,
Remember the Wolf is a hunter – go forth and get
    food of thine own.

Keep peace with the Lords of the Jungle – the
    Tiger, the Panther, the Bear;
And trouble not Hathi the Silent, and mock not
    the Boar in his lair.

When Pack meets with Pack in the Jungle, and
    neither will go from the trail,
Lie down till the leaders have spoken – it may be
    fair words shall prevail.

When ye fight with a Wolf of the Pack, ye must
    fight him alone and afar,
Lest others take part in the quarrel, and the Pack
    be diminished by war.

The Lair of the Wolf is his refuge, and where he
    has made him his home,
Not even the Head Wolf may enter, not even the
    Council may come.

The Lair of the Wolf is his refuge, but where he
    has digged it too plain,
The Council shall send him a message, and so he
    shall change it again.

If ye kill before midnight, be silent, and wake not
    the woods with your bay,
Lest ye frighten the deer from the crops, and the
    brothers go empty away.

Ye may kill for yourselves, and your mates, and
    your cubs as they need, and ye can;
But kill not for pleasure of killing, and *seven times
    never kill Man!*

If ye plunder his Kill from a weaker, devour not
    all in thy pride;
Pack-Right is the right of the meanest; so leave
    him the head and the hide.

The Kill of the Pack is the meat of the Pack. Ye
    must eat where it lies;
And no one may carry away of that meat to his
    lair, or he dies.

The Kill of the Wolf is the meat of the Wolf. He
    may do what he will,
But, till he has given permission, the Pack may
    not eat of that Kill.

Cub-Right is the right of the Yearling. From all of
    his Pack he may claim
Full-gorge when the killer has eaten; and none
    may refuse him the same.

Lair-Right is the right of the Mother. From all of
    her year she may claim
One haunch of each kill for her litter; and none
    may deny her the same.

Cave-Right is the right of the Father – to hunt by
    himself for his own:
He is freed of all calls to the Pack; he is judged by
    the Council alone.

Because of his age and his cunning, because of his
    gripe and his paw,
In all that the Law leaveth open, the word of the
    Head Wolf is Law.

Now these are the Laws of the Jungle, and many and
    mighty are they;
But the head and the hoof of the Law and the haunch
    and the hump is – Obey!

'How Fear Came' from *The Second Jungle Book*

The Children's Song

Puck of Pook's Hill

Land of our Birth, we pledge to thee
Our love and toil in the years to be;
When we are grown and take our place
As men and women with our race.

Father in Heaven who lovest all,
Oh, help Thy children when they call;
That they may build from age to age
An undefilèd heritage.

Teach us to bear the yoke in youth,
With steadfastness and careful truth;
That, in our time, Thy Grace may give
The Truth whereby the Nations live.

Teach us to rule ourselves alway,
Controlled and cleanly night and day;
That we may bring, if need arise,
No maimed or worthless sacrifice.

Teach us to look in all our ends
On Thee for judge, and not our friends;
That we, with Thee, may walk uncowed
By fear or favour of the crowd.

Teach us the Strength that cannot seek,
By deed or thought, to hurt the weak;
That, under Thee, we may possess
Man's strength to comfort man's distress.

Teach us Delight in simple things,
And Mirth that has no bitter springs;
Forgiveness free of evil done,
And Love to all men 'neath the sun!

Land of our Birth, our faith, our pride,
For whose dear sake our fathers died;
Oh, Motherland, we pledge to thee
Head, heart, and hand through the years to be!

If —

If you can keep your head when all about you
   Are losing theirs and blaming it on you,
If you can trust yourself when all men doubt you,
   But make allowance for their doubting too;
If you can wait and not be tired by waiting,
   Or being lied about, don't deal in lies,
Or being hated, don't give way to hating,
   And yet don't look too good, nor talk too wise:

If you can dream – and not make dreams your
     master,
   If you can think – and not make thoughts your
     aim;
If you can meet with Triumph and Disaster
   And treat those two impostors just the same;
If you can bear to hear the truth you've spoken
   Twisted by knaves to make a trap for fools,
Or watch the things you gave your life to, broken,
   And stoop and build 'em up with worn-out
     tools:

If you can make one heap of all your winnings
   And risk it on one turn of pitch-and-toss,
And lose, and start again at your beginnings
   And never breathe a word about your loss;
If you can force your heart and nerve and sinew
   To serve your turn long after they are gone,
And so hold on when there is nothing in you
   Except the Will which says to them: 'Hold on!'

If you can talk with crowds and keep your virtue,
    Or walk with Kings – nor lose the common
      touch,
If neither foes nor loving friends can hurt you,
    If all men count with you, but none too much;
If you can fill the unforgiving minute
    With sixty seconds' worth of distance run,
Yours is the Earth and everything that's in it,
    And – which is more – you'll be a Man, my son!

'Brother Square-Toes' in *Rewards and Fairies*

Philadelphia

If you're off to Philadelphia in the morning,
   You mustn't take my stories for a guide.
There's little left, indeed, of the city you will read
     of,
   And all the folk I write about have died.

Now few will understand if you mention Talleyrand,
   Or remember what his cunning and his skill did;
And the cabmen at the wharf do not know Count
     Zinzendorf,
   Nor the Church in Philadelphia he builded.

     It is gone, gone, gone with lost Atlantis,
     (Never say I didn't give you warning).
     In Seventeen Ninety-three 'twas there for all
        to see,
     But it's not in Philadelphia this morning.

If you're off to Philadelphia in the morning,
   You mustn't go by anything I've said.
Bob Bicknell's Southern Stages have been laid
     aside for ages,
   But the Limited will take you there instead.
Toby Hirte can't be seen at One Hundred and
     Eighteen
   North Second Street – no matter when you call;
And I fear you'll search in vain for the wash-house
     down the lane
   Where Pharaoh played the fiddle at the ball.

     It is gone, gone, gone with Thebes the Golden,
     (Never say I didn't give you warning).
     In Seventeen Ninety-four 'twas a famous
        dancing floor –
     But it's not in Philadelphia this morning.

If you're off to Philadelphia in the morning,
  You must telegraph for rooms at some Hotel.
You needn't try your luck at Epply's or 'The Buck,'
  Though the Father of his Country liked them
    well.
It is not the slightest use to inquire for Adam
    Goos,
  Or to ask where Pastor Meder has removed – so
You must treat as out of date the story I relate
  Of the Church in Philadelphia he loved so.

    He is gone, gone, gone with Martin Luther
      (Never say I didn't give you warning).
    In Seventeen Ninety-five he was (rest his
        soul!) alive,
    But he's not in Philadelphia this morning.

If you're off to Philadelphia this morning,
  And wish to prove the truth of what I say,
I pledge my word you'll find the pleasant land
    behind
  Unaltered since Red Jacket rode that way.
Still the pine-woods scent the noon; still the
    catbird sings his tune;
  Still autumn sets the maple-forest blazing;
Still the grapevine through the dusk flings her
    soul-compelling musk;
  Still the fireflies in the corn make night amazing!

    They are there, there, there with Earth
        immortal
      (Citizens, I give you friendly warning).
    The things that truly last when men and
        times have passed,
    They are all in Pennsylvania this morning!

'Brother Square-Toes' in *Rewards and Fairies*

Just So Verses

When the cabin portholes are dark and green
  Because of the seas outside;
When the ship goes *wop* (with a wiggle between)
And the steward falls into the soup-tureen,
  And the trunks begin to slide;
When Nursey lies on the floor in a heap,
And Mummy tells you to let her sleep,
And you aren't waked or washed or dressed,
Why, then you will know (if you haven't guessed)
You're 'Fifty North and Forty West!'
                    How the Whale Got his Throat

The Camel's hump is an ugly lump
  Which well you may see at the Zoo;
But uglier yet is the hump we get
  From having too little to do.

Kiddies and grownups too–oo–oo,
If we haven't enough to do–oo–oo,
        We get the hump –
        Cameelious hump –
The hump that is black and blue!

We climb out of bed with a frouzly head,
        And a snarly-yarly voice.
We shiver and scowl and we grunt and we growl
        At our bath and our boots and our toys;

And there ought to be a corner for me
(And I know there is one for you)
        When we get the hump –
        Cameelious hump –
The hump that is black and blue!

The cure for this ill is not to sit still,
   Or frowst with a book by the fire;
But to take a large hoe and a shovel also,
   And dig till you gently perspire;

And then you will find that the sun and the wind,
And the Djinn of the Garden too,
   Have lifted the hump –
   The horrible hump –
The hump that is black and blue!

I get it as well as you–oo–oo –
If I haven't enough to do–oo–oo!
   We all get hump –
   Cameelious hump –
Kiddies and grownups too!

     How the Camel Got his Hump

I am the Most Wise Baviaan, saying in most wise
  tones,
'Let us melt into the landscape – just us two by
  our lones.'
People have come – in a carriage – calling. But
  Mummy is there . . .
Yes, I can go if you take me – Nurse says *she* don't
  care.
Let's go up to the pig-styes and sit on the farm-
  yard rails!
Let's say things to the bunnies, and watch 'em
  skitter their tails!
Let's – oh, *anything*, daddy, so long as it's you and
  me,
And going truly exploring, and not being in till tea!

Here's your boots (I've brought 'em), and here's
    your cap and stick,
And here's your pipe and tobacco. Oh, come
    along out of it – quick!

How the Leopard Got his Spots

I keep six honest serving-men
    (They taught me all I knew);
Their names are What and Why and When
    And How and Where and Who.
I send them over land and sea,
    I send them east and west;
But after they have worked for me.
    I give them all a rest.

I let them rest from nine till five,
    For I am busy then,
As well as breakfast, lunch, and tea,
    For they are hungry men.
But different folk have different views.
    I know a person small –
She keeps ten million serving-men,
    Who get no rest at all!

She sends 'em abroad on her own affairs,
    From the second she opens her eyes –
One million Hows, two million Wheres,
    And seven million Whys!

The Elephant's Child

This is the mouth-filling song of the race that was
    run by a Boomer.
Run in a single burst – only event of its kind –
Started by Big God Nqong from Warrigaborriga-
    rooma,
Old Man Kangaroo first, Yellow-Dog Dingo
    behind.

Kangaroo bounded away, his back-legs working
    like pistons –
Bounded from morning till dark, twenty-five feet
    at a bound.
Yellow-Dog Dingo lay like a yellow cloud in the
    distance –
Much too busy to bark. My! but they covered the
    ground!

Nobody knows where they went, or followed the
    track that they flew in,
For that Continent hadn't been given a name.
They ran thirty degrees, from Torres Straits to the
    Leeuwin
(Look at the Atlas, please), then they ran back as
    they came.

S'posing you could trot from Adelaide to the Pacific,
For an afternoon's run – half what these gentlemen
    did –
You would feel rather hot, but your legs would
    develop terrific –
Yes, my importunate son, you'd be a Marvellous
    Kid!

    The Sing-Song of Old Man Kangaroo

I've never sailed the Amazon,
   I've never reached Brazil;
But the *Don* and *Magdalena*,
   They can go there when they will!

> Yes, weekly from Southampton,
> Great steamers, white and gold,
> Go rolling down to Rio
> (Roll down – roll down to Rio!).
> And I'd like to roll to Rio
> Some day before I'm old!

I've never seen a Jaguar,
   Nor yet an Armadill-
o dilloing in his armour,
   And I s'pose I never will,

> Unless I go to Rio
> These wonders to behold –
> Roll down – roll down to Rio –
> Roll really down to Rio!
> Oh, I'd love to roll to Rio
> Some day before I'm old!
>
> *The Beginning of the Armadilloes*

China-going P.&O.s
Pass Pau Amma's playground close,
And his Pusat Tasek lies
Near the track of most B.I.s.
N.Y.K. and N.D.L.
Know Pau Amma's home as well
As the Fisher of the Sea knows
'Bens,' M.M.s and Rubattinos.
But (and this is rather queer)
A.T.L.s can not come here;
O. and O. and D.O.A.
Must go round another way.
Orient, Anchor, Bibby, Hall,
Never go that way at all.
U.C.S. would have a fit
If it found itself on it.
And if 'Beavers' took their cargoes
To Penang instead of Lagos,
Or a fat Shaw-Savill bore
Passengers to Singapore,
Or a White Star were to try a
Little trip to Sourabaya,
Or a B.S.A. went on
Past Natal to Cheribon,
Then great Mr Lloyds would come
With a wire and drag them home!

*　　　*　　　*

You'll know what my riddle means
When you've eaten mangosteens.
The Crab that Played with the Sea

Pussy can sit by the fire and sing,
  Pussy can climb a tree,
Or play with a silly old cork and string
  To 'muse herself, not me.
But *I* like *Binkie* my dog, because
  He knows how to behave;
So, *Binkie's* the same as the First Friend was,
  And I am the Man in the Cave!

Pussy will play Man-Friday till
  It's time to wet her paw
And make her walk on the window-sill
  (For the footprint Crusoe saw);
Then she fluffles her tail and mews,
  And scratches and won't attend.
But *Binkie* will play whatever I choose,
  And he is my true First Friend!

Pussy will rub my knees with her head
  Pretending she loves me hard;
But the very minute I go to my bed
  Pussy runs out in the yard,
And there she stays till the morning-light;
  So I know it is only pretend;
But *Binkie*, he snores at my feet all night,
  And he is my Firstest Friend!
                    The Cat that Walked by Himself

This Uninhabited Island
 Is near Cape Gardafui;
But it's hot – too hot – off Suez
 For the likes of you and me
Ever to go in a P.&O.
 To call on the Cake Parsee.
How the Rhinoceros got his Skin

There was never a Queen like Balkis,
 From here to the wide world's end;
But Balkis talked to a butterfly
 As you would talk to a friend.

There was never a King like Solomon,
 Not since the world began;
But Solomon talked to a butterfly
 As a man would talk to a man.

She was Queen of Sabaea –
 And *he* was Asia's Lord –
But they both of 'em talked to butterflies
 When they took their walks abroad!
The Butterfly that Stamped

Mine Sweepers

Sea Warfare

Dawn off the Foreland – the young flood making
  Jumbled and short and steep –
Black in the hollows and bright where it's
     breaking –
   Awkward water to sweep.
   'Mines reported in the fairway,
   Warn all traffic and detain.
'Sent up *Unity, Claribel, Assyrian, Stormcock*, and
   Golden Gain.'

Noon off the Foreland – the first ebb making
  Lumpy and strong in the bight.
Boom after boom, and the golf-hut shaking
  And the jackdaws wild with fright!
   'Mines located in the fairway,
   Boats now working up the chain,
Sweepers – *Unity, Claribel, Assyrian, Stormcock*,
   and *Golden Gain*.'

Dusk off the Foreland – the last light going
  And the traffic crowding through,
And five damned trawlers with their syreens
     blowing
   Heading the whole review!
   'Sweep completed in the fairway.
   No more mines remain.
'Sent back *Unity, Claribel, Assyrian, Stormcock*,
   and *Golden Gain*.'

1914–18

'The Trade'

Sea Warfare

They bear, in place of classic names,
    Letters and numbers on their skin.
They play their grisly blindfold games
    In little boxes made of tin.
    Sometimes they stalk the Zeppelin,
Sometimes they learn where mines are laid,
    Or where the Baltic ice is thin.
That is the custom of 'The Trade.'

Few prize-courts sit upon their claims.
    They seldom tow their targets in.
They follow certain secret aims
    Down under, far from strife or din.
    When they are ready to begin
No flag is flown, no fuss is made
    More than the shearing of a pin.
That is the custom of 'The Trade.'

The Scout's quadruple funnel flames
    A mark from Sweden to the Swin,
The Cruiser's thund'rous screw proclaims
    Her comings out and goings in:
    But only whiffs of paraffin
Or creamy rings that fizz and fade
    Show where the one-eyed Death has been.
That is the custom of 'The Trade.'

Their feats, their fortunes and their fames
    Are hidden from their nearest kin;
No eager public backs or blames,
    No journal prints the yarn they spin

(The Censor would not let it in!)
When they return from run or raid.
Unheard they work, unseen they win.
That is the custom of 'The Trade.'

1914–18

A Smuggler's Song

If you wake at midnight, and hear a horse's feet,
Don't go drawing back the blind, or looking in the
    street,
Them that asks no questions isn't told a lie.
Watch the wall, my darling, while the Gentlemen
    go by!
       Five and twenty ponies
       Trotting through the dark –
       Brandy for the Parson,
       'Baccy for the Clerk;
       Laces for a lady, letters for a spy,
And watch the wall, my darling, while the Gentle-
    men go by!

Running round the woodlump if you chance to find
Little barrels, roped and tarred, all full of brandy-
    wine,
Don't you shout to come and look, nor use 'em
    for your play.
Put the brishwood back again – and they'll be
    gone next day!

If you see the stable-door setting open wide;
If you see a tired horse lying down inside;
If your mother mends a coat cut about and tore;
If the lining's wet and warm – don't you ask no
    more!

If you meet King George's men, dressed in blue
    and red,
You be careful what you say, and mindful what is
    said.

If they call you 'pretty maid,' and chuck you
      'neath the chin,
Don't you tell where no one is, nor yet where no
      one's been!

Knocks and footsteps round the house – whistles
      after dark –
You've no call for running out till the house-dogs
      bark.
Trusty's here, and *Pincher's* here, and see how
      dumb they lie –
They don't fret to follow when the Gentlemen go by!

If you do as you've been told, 'likely there's a
      chance,
You'll be give a dainty doll, all the way from France,
With a cap of Valenciennes, and a velvet hood –
A present from the Gentlemen, along o' being good!
      Five and twenty ponies
      Trotting through the dark –
      Brandy for the Parson,
      'Baccy for the Clerk.
Them that asks no questions isn't told a lie –
Watch the wall, my darling, while the Gentlemen
      go by!

      'Hal o' the Draft' in *Puck of Pook's Hill*

The Roman Centurion's Song

Roman Occupation of Britain, A.D. 300

Legate, I had the news last night – my cohort
    ordered home
By ship to Portus Itius and thence by road to Rome.
I've marched the companies aboard, the arms are
    stowed below:
Now let another take my sword. Command me
    not to go!

I've served in Britain forty years, from Vectis to
    the Wall.
I have none other home than this, nor any life at all.
Last night I did not understand, but, now the
    hour draws near
That calls me to my native land, I feel that land is
    here.

Here where men say my name was made, here
    where my work was done;
Here where my dearest dead are laid – my wife –
    my wife and son;
Here where time, custom, grief and toil, age,
    memory, service, love,
Have rooted me in British soil. Ah, how can I
    remove?

For me this land, that sea, these airs, those folk
    and fields suffice.
What purple Southern pomp can match our
    changeful Northern skies,
Black with December snows unshed or pearled
    with August haze –
The clanging arch of steel-grey March, or June's
    long-lighted days?

You'll follow widening Rhodanus till vine and
olive lean
Aslant before the sunny breeze that sweeps
Nemausus clean
To Arelate's triple gate; but let me linger on,
Here where our stiff-necked British oaks confront
Euroclydon!

You'll take the old Aurelian Road through shore-
descending pines
Where, blue as any peacock's neck, the Tyrrhene
Ocean shines.
You'll go where laurel crowns are won, but – will
you e'er forget
The scent of hawthorn in the sun, or bracken in
the wet?

Let me work here for Britain's sake – at any task
you will –
A marsh to drain, a road to make or native troops
to drill.
Some Western camp (I know the Pict) or granite
Border keep,
Mid seas of heather derelict, where our old
messmates sleep.

Legate, I come to you in tears – My cohort
ordered home!
I've served in Britain forty years. What should I
do in Rome?
Here is my heart, my soul, my mind – the only life
I know.
I cannot leave it all behind. Command me not to
go!

Dane-geld

A.D. *980–1016*

It is always a temptation to an armed and agile
   nation
      To call upon a neighbour and to say: –
'We invaded you last night – we are quite prepared
   to fight,
      Unless you pay us cash to go away.'

And that is called asking for Dane-geld,
      And the people who ask it explain
That you've only to pay 'em the Dane-geld
      And then you'll get rid of the Dane!

It is always a temptation to a rich and lazy nation,
      To puff and look important and to say: –
'Though we know we should defeat you, we have
   not the time to meet you.
      We will therefore pay you cash to go away.'

And that is called paying the Dane-geld;
      But we've proved it again and again,
That if once you have paid him the Dane-geld
      You never get rid of the Dane.

It is wrong to put temptation in the path of any
   nation,
      For fear they should succumb and go astray;
So when you are requested to pay up or be
   molested,
      You will find it better policy to say: –

'We never pay *any*-one Dane-geld,
      No matter how trifling the cost;
For the end of that game is oppression and shame,
      And the nation that plays it is lost!'

James I

1603–25

The child of Mary Queen of Scots,
  A shifty mother's shiftless son,
Bred up among intrigues and plots,
  Learnèd in all things, wise in none.
Ungainly, babbling, wasteful, weak,
  Shrewd, clever, cowardly, pedantic,
The sight of steel would blanch his cheek
  The smell of baccy drive him frantic.
He was the author of his line –
  He wrote that witches should be burnt;
He wrote that monarchs were divine,
  And left a son who – proved they weren't!

Edgehill Fight

Civil Wars, 1642

Naked and grey the Cotswolds stand
  Beneath the autumn sun,
And the stubble-fields on either hand
  Where Stour and Avon run.
There is no change in the patient land
  That has bred us every one.

She should have passed in cloud and fire
  And saved us from this sin
Of war – red war – 'twixt child and sire,
  Household and kith and kin,
In the heart of a sleepy Midland shire,
  With the harvest scarcely in.

But there is no change as we meet at last
  On the brow-head or the plain,
And the raw astonished ranks stand fast
  To slay or to be slain
By the men they knew in the kindly past
  That shall never come again –

By the men they met at dance or chase,
  In the tavern or the hall,
At the justice-bench and the marketplace,
  At the cudgel-play or brawl –
Of their own blood and speech and race,
  Comrades or neighbours all!

More bitter than death this day must prov
  Whichever way it go,

For the brothers of the maids we love
   Make ready to lay low
Their sisters' sweethearts, as we move
   Against our dearest foe.

Thank Heaven! At last the trumpets peal
   Before our strength gives way.
For King or for the Commonweal –
   No matter which they say,
The first dry rattle of new-drawn steel
   Changes the world today!

The Dutch in the Medway

1664–72

If wars were won by feasting,
  Or victory by song,
Or safely found in sleeping sound,
  How England would be strong!
But honour and dominion
  Are not maintainèd so.
They're only got by sword and shot,
  And this the Dutchmen know!

The moneys that should feed us
  You spend on your delight,
How can you then have sailor-men
  To aid you in your fight?
Our fish and cheese are rotten,
  Which makes the scurvy grow –
We cannot serve you if we starve,
  And this the Dutchmen know!

Our ships in every harbour
  Be neither whole nor sound,
And, when we seek to mend a leak,
  No oakum can be found;
Or, if it is, the caulkers,
  And carpenters also,
For lack of pay have gone away,
  And this the Dutchmen know!

Mere powder, guns, and bullets,
  We scarce can get at all;
Their price was spent in merriment

And revel at Whitehall,
While we in tattered doublets
    From ship to ship must row,
Beseeching friends for odds and ends –
    And this the Dutchmen know!

No King will heed our warnings,
    No Court will pay our claims –
Our King and Court for their disport
    Do sell the very Thames!
For, now De Ruyter's topsails
    Off naked Chatham show,
We dare not meet him with our fleet –
    And this the Dutchmen know!

Big Steamers

'Oh, Where are you going to, all you Big Steamers
    With England's own coal, up and down the
    salt seas?'
'We are going to fetch you your bread and your
    butter,
    Your beef, pork, and mutton, eggs, apples,
    and cheese.'

'And where will you fetch it from, all you Big
    Steamers,
    And where shall I write you when you are
    away?'
'We fetch it from Melbourne, Quebec, and
    Vancouver –
    Address us at Hobart, Hong-Kong, and
    Bombay.'

'But if anything happened to all you Big Steamers,
    And suppose you were wrecked up and down
    the salt sea?'
'Then you'd have no coffee or bacon for breakfast,
    And you'd have no muffins or toast for your
    tea.'

'Then I'll pray for fine weather for all you Big
    Steamers,
    For little blue billows and breezes so soft.'
'Oh, billows and breezes don't bother Big Steamers,
    For we're iron below and steel-rigging aloft.'

Then I'll build a new lighthouse for all you Big
  Steamers,
    With plenty wise pilots to pilot you through.'
Oh, the Channel's as bright as a ballroom already,
    And pilots are thicker than pilchards at Looe.'

Then what can I do for you, all you Big Steamers,
    Oh, what can I do for your comfort and good?'
Send out your big warships to watch your big
  waters,
    That no one may stop us from bringing you
      food.

For the bread that you eat and the biscuits you nibble,
    The sweets that you suck and the joints that you
      carve,
They are brought to you daily by all us Big Steamers –
    And if any one hinders our coming you'll starve!

                                    1914–18

The Glory of the Garden

Our England is a garden that is full of stately views
Of borders, beds and shrubberies and lawns and
    avenues,
With statues on the terraces and peacocks
    strutting by;
But the Glory of the Garden lies in more than
    meets the eye.

For where the old thick laurels grow, along the
    thin red wall,
You find the tool- and potting-sheds which are
    the heart of all;
The cold-frames and the hot-houses, the dungpits
    and the tanks,
The rollers, carts and drainpipes, with the arrows
    and the planks.

And there you'll see the gardeners, the men and
    'prentice boys
Told off to do as they are bid and do it without
    noise;
For, except when seeds are planted and we shout
    to scare the birds,
The Glory of the Garden it abideth not in words.

And some can pot begonias and some can bud a
    rose,
And some are hardly fit to trust with anything that
    grows;
But they can roll and trim the lawns and sift the
    sand and loam,
For the Glory of the Garden occupieth all who
    come.

Our England is a garden, and such gardens are
 not made
By singing: – 'Oh, how beautiful!' and sitting in
 the shade,
While better men than we go out and start their
 working lives
At grubbing weeds from gravel-paths with broken
 dinner-knives.

There's not a pair of legs so thin, there's not a
 head so thick,
There's not a hand so weak and white, nor yet a
 heart so sick,
But it can find some needful job that's crying to
 be done,
For the Glory of the Garden glorifieth every one.

Then seek your job with thankfulness and work
 till further orders,
If it's only netting strawberries or killing slugs on
 borders;
And when your back stops aching and your hands
 begin to harden,
You will find yourself a partner in the Glory of the
 Garden.

Oh, Adam was a gardener, and God who made
 him sees
That half a proper gardener's work is done upon
 his knees,
So when your work is finished, you can wash your
 hands and pray
For the Glory of the Garden, that it may not pass
 away!
And the Glory of the Garden it shall never pass away!

The Gods of the Copybook Headings

As I pass through my incarnations in every age
and race,
I make my proper prostrations to the Gods of the
Market Place.
Peering through reverent fingers I watch them
flourish and fall,
And the Gods of the Copybook Headings, I
notice, outlast them all.

We were living in trees when they met us. They
showed us each in turn
That Water would certainly wet us, as Fire would
certainly burn:
But we found them lacking in Uplift, Vision and
Breadth of Mind,
So we left them to teach the Gorillas while we
followed the March of Mankind.

We moved as the Spirit listed. *They* never altered
their pace,
Being neither cloud nor wind-borne like the Gods
of the Marketplace;
But they always caught up with our progress, and
presently word would come
That a tribe had been wiped off its icefield, or the
lights had gone out in Rome.

With the Hopes that our World is built on they
were utterly out of touch,
They denied that the Moon was Stilton; they
denied she was even Dutch.

They denied that Wishes were Horses; they
   denied that a Pig had Wings.
So we worshipped the Gods of the Market Who
   promised these beautiful things.

When the Cambrian measures were forming,
   They promised perpetual peace.
They swore, if we gave them our weapons, that
   the wars of the tribes would cease.
But when we disarmed They sold us and delivered
   us bound to our foe,
And the Gods of the Copybook Headings said:
   'Stick to the Devil you know.'

On the first Feminian Sandstones we were
   promised the Fuller Life
(Which started by loving our neighbour and
   ended by loving his wife)
Till our women had no more children and the
   men lost reason and faith,
And the Gods of the Copybook Headings said:
   'The Wages of Sin is Death.'

In the Carboniferous Epoch we were promised
   abundance for all,
By robbing selected Peter to pay for collective
   Paul;
But, though we had plenty of money, there was
   nothing our money could buy,
And the Gods of the Copybook Headings said: *'If
   you don't work you die.'*

295

Then the Gods of the Market tumbled, and their
    smooth-tongued wizards withdrew,
And the hearts of the meanest were humbled and
    began to believe it was true
That All is not Gold that Glitters, and Two and
    Two make Four –
And the Gods of the Copybook Headings limped
    up to explain it once more.

       *   *   *

As it will be in the future, it was at the birth of
    Man –
There are only four things certain since Social
    Progress began: –
That the Dog returns to his Vomit and the Sow
    returns to her Mire,
And the burnt Fool's bandaged finger goes
    wabbling back to the Fire;

And that after this is accomplished, and the brave
    new world begins
When all men are paid for existing and no man
    must pay for his sins,
As surely as Water will wet us, as surely as Fire
    will burn,
The Gods of the Copybook Headings with terror
    and slaughter return!

1919

The Storm Cone

This is the midnight – let no star
Delude us – dawn is very far.
This is the tempest long foretold –
Slow to make head but sure to hold

Stand by! The lull 'twixt blast and blast
Signals the storm is near, not past;
And worse than present jeopardy
May our forlorn tomorrow be.

If we have cleared the expectant reef,
Let no man look for his relief.
Only the darkness hides the shape
Of further peril to escape.

It is decreed that we abide
The weight of gale against the tide
And those huge waves the outer main
Sends in to set us back again.

They fall and whelm. We strain to hear
The pulses of her labouring gear,
Till the deep throb beneath us proves,
After each shudder and check, she moves!

She moves, with all save purpose lost,
To make her offing from the coast;
But, till she fetches open sea,
Let no man deem that he is free!

1932

The Appeal

IF I HAVE GIVEN YOU DELIGHT
BY AUGHT THAT I HAVE DONE,
LET ME LIE QUIET IN THAT NIGHT
WHICH SHALL BE YOURS ANON:

AND FOR THE LITTLE, LITTLE, SPAN
THE DEAD ARE BORNE IN MIND,
SEEK NOT TO QUESTION OTHER THAN
THE BOOKS I LEAVE BEHIND.

Index of Poems

Index of First Lines